A Horror Story

MILLER'S RIDGE

WILL MULLINS

This is a work of fiction. Names, characters, places, and incidents are products of the author's imagination or are used fictitiously and are not to be construed as real. Any resemblance to actual events, locations, organizations, or persons, living or dead, is entirely coincidental.

World Castle Publishing, LLC
Pensacola, Florida
Copyright © Will Mullins 2023
Paperback ISBN: 9781960076885
eBook ISBN: 9781960076892
First Edition World Castle Publishing, LLC, June 19, 2023
http://www.worldcastlepublishing.com
Licensing Notes
Cover: Karen Fuller
Editor: Karen Fuller

CHAPTER 1

Vanessa worried for the future of her newborn daughter as she made her way through the woods on the outskirts of town, the scents of poplar and fallen leaves failing to provide the comfort they had offered her frequently in the past. The night before had been devoid of restful sleep. In her dreams, she had ridden dark torrents across a Stygian channel in a ship born of bone and seeming chaos. Her visions were never entirely clear, but that she and her daughter were both at risk seemed a forgone conclusion as the branches of lofty and ancient trees towered above her, ominous specters foretelling some unseen danger on the horizon. Vanessa dreaded her emergence from the forest's shade, foreboding though it may have seemed at the moment. She would meet with the old man upon exiting these woods.

Her experiences with him were growing increasingly disturbing. He and his kind wanted something more from her than she was willing to give, more than she could possibly part with. She didn't know if they had grown in might or merely in audacity. There were rumors of them in the backwoods, whispered words that suggested there might be no limit to their strange powers. Vanessa had heard such stories from childhood, at least when she was among those who shunned the outside world. She maintained a healthy respect for the old man and those like him, but she wouldn't believe the fancies of the deep woods folk who simply needed superstitious stories with which to occupy their days and nights. She would talk to Jarret, set him straight once and for all, then be on her way back to town. Vanessa had an entirely new life planned for herself and her child, one that would leave far behind the likes of Jarret.

Vanessa stepped out from beneath the

canopy of branches above, emerging beside a back road that led to popular campsites used by those who were trying to get away from their fast-paced lives, the kind of life she intended to begin when she moved out of the Appalachian mountains and into a place in the city. Everything was set. She and her daughter would move and start everything anew within the month. It was all she thought about.

Her eyes landed on the old country store across the road. She strolled toward it, so occupied with thoughts of the future that she failed to notice a cloaked figure standing nearby in the woods. The figure observed her, dispassionate in his stance, as she completed her trek to the country store and entered. As she walked inside, three other mysterious figures joined the first, waiting and watching.

Vanessa strolled casually through the store, nodding at a young cashier who barely acknowledged her presence. He seemed more interested in watching the college football game on the wall-mounted television than paying any attention to potential customers. She supposed she couldn't blame him since she was the only person potentially falling into that category at the moment, and indeed, she was not there to make a purchase.

Stepping into the back room, it felt as if she had walked through a web, something gossamer fine stroking her pale skin and long blonde hair. She saw nothing. Perhaps her nerves were unsettled, causing a physiological reaction as she approached the conversation she dreaded. She saw Jarret then, sitting behind a small table in the process of lifting a cup of coffee to his lips. The wall behind him was covered in icons and images that represented a blend of Celtic, Middle Eastern, and Native American ancestry and spiritual beliefs.

Jarret was more complicated than his exterior would imply. He was a weathered but tough looking man in his sixties, tall and broad shouldered. He wore a simple flannel shirt and a pair of old glasses. A fine white whisp was all that remained of his hair. He looked at her pleasantly enough as she entered and gestured for her to sit down across from him.

She did so, wondering suddenly if it had been a mistake to even agree to meet with him after the peculiar conversations he and his kind had lured her into of late. Well, there was nothing she could do about it now. She would allow him to say his peace.

"Have some coffee, girl." Jarret greeted her with his gruff voice, producing a guttural utterance that highlighted the rugged sort of man he was. Emerging from anyone else's mouth, the clipped introduction might have seemed mildly condescending but not nearly so annoying as she found it to be in his case. He pushed a mug across the table in her direction.

"I didn't come here for coffee. I came to find out what you want from me."

Jarret issued a curt, vaguely disturbing chuckle. He straightened up in his seat. "We'll get straight to it then. I saved you from prison, girl. You'd be there right now if it weren't for me."

Without missing a beat, she responded, "And what is it you're wanting?"

He gave her a look that suggested she already well knew what he wanted, but he proceeded with an explanation all the same. "Did you know your child is a born seer?"

"What!? What does Laura have to do with this? I've told you I don't want you people around her. I'm not willing to let you turn her into one of your followers like she's some kind of experiment. She's a child, not a lab rat."

"She will walk lost somewhere between this world and the next. As the years pass, she will wake up to this power within her." Jarret spoke the words calmly and with complete conviction, so much so that Vanessa was taken aback by them. In that moment, his sincerity frightened her deeply. What if he was right?

"My daughter will have nothing to do with you and your kind."

Jarret issued an ironic laugh that chilled her deep down within at the very center of her being. He then leaned across the table to look Vanessa directly in the eyes.

"You can't stop it. I can't stop it. She is one of us. Let me protect her before the darker elements lay claim to her."

"No. I'm taking my daughter and getting off of this mountain. End of story. I don't know who is the darker element, you or someone else. I'm not sticking around to find out, and my child isn't going to be the plaything of your warped beliefs."

Vanessa stood and made her way toward the door.

"Girl, it won't work. It's too late for that. I'm your only hope… her only hope."

"We'll see about that, old man." With that, Vanessa stormed out of the room, through the store beyond, and back outside. She couldn't believe she had bothered to meet with him. It was time to take the shortcut back to her place, grab her daughter, and leave before any of these lunatics did something to harm her family.

* * *

Later that night, in the pitch darkness, Vanessa lay on the cold ground by a small rustic cabin lost somewhere in the midst of the surrounding wilderness. All was silent and seemingly devoid of life. She was dying, blood draining from numerous wounds to her back and chest. A pool of it was forming beneath her, causing her fine hair to adhere to the grass as her brown eyes stared at the night sky.

As she took her final breaths, Vanessa heard an unknown woman's voice in her mind…

or was it on the very breeze? The woman spoke as if reading a poem, the theme of which was sobering and dark. Yet, there was an odd hint of hopefulness and life in her voice.

Why does death never lie about?
Is it not listless on occasion,
disenchanted with its work,
disillusioned with the society of the departed?
Its stride is insidious constancy.
So many pass in this unchanging action,
yet the journey is always made alone.
Would not the blow be softened,
if we sat in a darkened cinema,
comfortable side by side in our chairs,
watched the screen fade to black,
and awakened to the second feature together?

CHAPTER 2

The path to Cullowdale College forms an exit from the modern world, a journey into the silent knowledge of a forest that was once home to unthinkable, forgotten magic. The people who inhabited the forest long before the arrival of Europeans and Middle Easterners were possessed with a greater awareness of the forest's mysteries and powers than the daily activities and obsessions of contemporary life allow for. Sometimes, they even interacted with beings born of the old world, but they were always aware of the boundary between the visible spectrum and what lies beyond. Always, they heard the whispering of spirits on the wind. After the daily setting of the sun, they passed through dreams rife with visions of the energetic potential of the good and evil forces inhabiting the ancient terrain.

Not far away from the college, in the high places, the spirits roam more freely. High on the mountainside, Vanessa had lived a tortured life and given birth to a girl who never really knew her mother or the source of her torment. But her daughter was bound to her mother's past in ways she had yet to fully understand.

* * *

Laura Morris ferried herself along in her vintage four-door sedan, passing through the valley in which her place of employment resided at a casual pace. The pace was casual because the culture of Cullowdale was equally so. The vehicle was vintage because her salary at the small college wouldn't allow for something new. That said, she enjoyed her work. Tranquility was the order of the day on campus with rare exceptions, and she was in a nearly autonomous role that provided her with ample time to read good books and sip hot beverages while on the proverbial clock. On certain occasions in the past, friends had attempted to recruit her for faster paced positions at universities or in the corporate world. Their pitches were met with a polite refusal. She did enjoy making her way out of Cullowdale from time to time, but why would she want to add stress to her life?

She pulled into her unofficial parking space and walked up to the small brick building that was home to her office. She thought of the many friends she had made on campus in just six years since graduating from college herself. Aside from other staff members, she had made friends with many of the students. It wasn't at all unnatural for a school counselor to do so. In fact, she was expecting a visit from a few of those students that very afternoon.

Laura settled into the comfortable leather-covered desk chair she had splurged on as a birthday gift for herself a couple of years earlier. It was an extravagant purchase, birthday or no, but she had little else to spend money on and spent about as much time in her office as she did at home in her tiny condominium. As she awaited the arrival of her young friends, she twirled her dirty blonde hair into loops with one finger and slowly typed responses to a few emails with her opposite hand. Laura was full of anxious energy despite her predilection for maintaining a casual pace in life. She constantly engaged in one seemingly nervous or distracted habit or another, from playing with her wispy hair to adjusting the glasses on her face just above her fierce cheekbones and below her warm brown eyes.

Just as she had nearly twirled her hair into a knot and managed to clear her inbox of any emails of importance, there was a single, chirpy knock at her office door. Without any further formality, the door swung open, and three familiar faces rushed in and planted their accompanying backsides on chairs near her desk.

All three of her sudden but expected visitors were students at Cullowdale. Karen, Theresa, and Alex were energetic youths that Laura had been privileged to become friends with over the course of the most recent school year.

Karen and Theresa were both blondes of average stature, somewhat differentiated in appearance by the strawberry highlights visible in Karen's mane of curly hair. Laura never was quite sure whether the tone of Karen's hair was natural or artificial, and she chose not to ask for discretion's sake... just as she chose not to inquire as to whether or not Theresa might spend a considerable amount of time in a tanning bed.

The two could further be distinguished by Karen's relatively formal manner of dressing for a college student. She was rarely seen without either a smartly matched polo and khakis or a nice dress, accompanied in either case by neat loafers or dress shoes. Theresa was more of a jeans and tee shirt kind of gal, frequently given to plodding about in well-worn sandals.

Alex leaned back in a chair between the two girls, stretching out his lanky form in the casual fashion of a college boy who believed himself well in control of the world around him. He wasn't cocky or extraordinarily self-confident, merely comfortable with his surroundings. He was a reed in the wind of sorts, skinny, floppy, and long-haired. He wore jeans and a golf shirt along with tennis shoes as if donning the official uniform of the male Cullowdale student body. Typically, it was too cold for shorts and too informal, even for khaki pants. At that moment, it was summer, but Alex stuck with the jeans.

The three of them had booked this time with Laura to plead with her to join them on a summer research trip to the mountains. Laura had rejected the offer initially due to both her uncertainty about how her superiors at the college might view her participation in the trip and her ambivalent feelings about spending time in the minimally populated mountain communities. She had been born on the side of a nearby mountain, and she had spent little time there since, just a few brief visits out of curiosity about her past. Most of her life had been spent in small nearby cities and in the series of valleys in which Cullowdale College stood.

Laura was first to break the noticeable silence after her guests reclined across from her. "Well, hello. You're a bit early."

The silence remained intact.

Laura grinned and continued, "Am I getting the silent treatment?" She knew that she was. She had experienced it before at the hands of these three.

Still, none of her visitors responded.

"I'll take that as a yes. And what can I do to remedy the situation?" Laura knew the answer but asked anyway. She actually enjoyed the silent treatment and drawing people out of it by asking the right questions. She was a trained counselor, after all.

Karen was the first to speak up, "Say yes."

"I see. It's as easy as that, is it?" Laura leaned forward and peered across the desk at the three of them with great seriousness. "Are you sure you guys want me along for this trip? Wouldn't you have more fun without the school counselor hanging around?"

"No. We're sure," replied Karen. She spoke with the type A variety of certainty for which she was known. Laura rarely expected anything else from her.

"Is Jason as sure as you are? I noticed he isn't here."

Alex piped up, "Oh. He's just taking an exam, or he would have come with us." Alex gave Theresa a knowing look and shrugged a bit.

Theresa groaned with a skeptical look on her face, "I don't know why. He didn't study. He's going to make like a twenty on it."

Karen covered her mouth with her hand and exchanged a quick glance with both of her young friends.

Alex didn't quite know what to think about this gesture and offered an incredulous look in response, "What?"

Karen answered, "We shouldn't even be talking. She hasn't said yes yet."

Laura leaned back in her chair and surveyed the students in front of her. Without drama, she shrugged, "Yes."

Upon hearing Laura agree to come along, Karen's mood grew all the more sanguine. "OK. We leave tomorrow morning. Pack light. There isn't a lot of room."

Laura relaxed in her chair, beginning to embrace the concept of getting away from the daily routine for a while. "And we're going to be gone for how long?"

Theresa was the first to offer her some details, "Two weeks, at least." She then looked to the others for agreement, and they nodded their heads "yes." Then, it was as if they exchanged some silent signal between themselves at the speed of a barely noticeable glance. Grins on their faces, they all stood up and began to walk out of the room without a further word.

Laura wasn't surprised by their conspiratorial behavior, but she wasn't about to let them simply walk out of the room in such a dismissive fashion. "Wait a minute! I don't get any further details? That's all of it?"

They all broke out laughing at her and halted their exit, turning around to face her at her desk.

Theresa spoke up, "There really isn't much else to tell. Silent treatment is officially revoked, but we don't have much to fill the silence with."

Laura didn't quite know how to respond to the level of disorganization, especially considering Karen's involvement with the planning. She searched for words and spoke gingerly when she found them, "OK. Do any of you know anything about paranormal research?"

Alex made it fairly clear that they didn't.

"No. Pretty much not anything...."

Laura continued her query, "So, what exactly is the plan?" She focused her gaze on Karen, hoping for a more lucid response from the known planner among their little group.

"We head up to the mountains, bounce around from one haunted place to the next, shoot some DV footage, take notes...." Karen began until interrupted by the sole male presence in the room.

"And if any actual ghosts show up, we promptly shit our pants," Alex offered in his less than helpful fashion.

"I will be leaving that particular reaction up to you, Alex. I mean, if that's the best you have to offer, please just be sure to bring a spare pair of, well, everything...," responded Laura, suddenly beginning to wonder whether she could properly tolerate two or more weeks of constant exposure to the undergraduate hi jinks.

Theresa brought the conversation back to some degree of productivity, "You've done this before. You should be the one giving us instructions."

Laura chuckled despite herself. She had

one minor experience with the paranormal years earlier when she was a student herself and had made the mistake of telling her Cullowdale friends about it. "It was no big deal, believe me. Just an overnight field trip with some of my college friends."

"But you saw something strange, didn't you?" asked Karen.

Laura brushed the whole thing off as best she could. "We did. But, I've barely even thought about it since."

"It's time to start thinking about it then," said Alex.

Once again, the three of them turned to leave Laura's office. This time, Karen bothered to say "Bye!" Alex and Theresa merely smiled and chuckled, already beginning to chat about exams on the way out.

A serious look made its way across Laura's face as her visitors disappeared from sight. She knew she hadn't been entirely truthful with them. What she had seen on that trip during her college years wasn't her only experience with the paranormal. There was more. Something that peered at her from hidden places, something she was afraid to encounter in its full force, waited for her, possibly high up in those mountains.

CHAPTER 3

Jason sat in his dorm room, waiting on Alex to return from his visit to their school counselor's office. Laura was one of those people who made them feel like they were valued and should already be impacting the world rather than playing the role of privileged kids who should just sit in the corner and be thankful they were young and getting to go to college. He supposed the confidence she inspired was the reason they all got excited about involving her in things that they wouldn't have asked anyone else from the faculty or staff to participate in. From his perspective, it didn't hurt that she wasn't bad to look at, either. Honestly, he didn't have a need to see beyond that and find any greater reason for wanting her along, not that he would even think about attempting to do anything other than look. There were enough college girls around, after all.

Positioned in front of his computer in the hot dorm room, he welcomed the end of exams and the imminent freedoms of the summer months and appropriately perspired in his nondescript sweatshirt. Stroking his fingers through his sandy hair, he peered at a rather odd series of images on his computer's monitor.

As he pondered the nature of what he had discovered, his roommate Alex strolled back into the room and made his way over to stand nearby.

"What's up?" greeted Jason as Alex moved through the small room.

"We just talked to Laura."

"Oh yeah. What did she say? What's her verdict on joining the beer swillers on their summer road trip? If you can call it that... personally, I'm starting to regret that this bus isn't pointed in the direction of warm sands and sunshine."

"I don't know about all that, but she's

going... to the mountains, that is...." Alex seemed pleased with their efforts as he walked over to the mini fridge and grabbed a can of cheap beer. "Want one?"

"Do you have to ask?"

Alex grabbed a second can of beer and walked over to hand it to Jason, plopping down on a chair near his friend and roommate. "What the blazes are you looking at anyway? Don't we already know where we're staying?"

"No. Check this out. I found this online last night."

"Does it have something to do with organic chemistry?"

Jason laughed and began draining the can of beer with a look on his face like life simply couldn't get much better. No. I studied for about fifteen minutes this morning."

Alex turned his can up as if in competition. "And how did that work for you?"

"Not so well," Jason responded in an indifferent fashion before pointing to the monitor in front of him.

"OK. I'll bite. So, what is this? You seem pretty darn excited about it. Just looks like a really crappy website to me." Alex was halfway through his can of beer by this point but still lagging behind Jason's remarkable beer-guzzling pace.

"It's a website called the direct dial compendium, or just the Compendium for short. Did you realize there are still tons of old-school bulletin board systems out there?"

"No, I didn't, considering I don't know what they are." Alex marveled at Jason's technical knowledge. He seemed to care nothing about his studies in general, blowing off almost all of his classes and assignments in favor of alternating between beer drinking and playing rugby or basketball. Yet, he had an innate skill for pretty much all things computer oriented that would serve him well after college. He didn't even take computer classes or hang out with the IT types. He simply learned it on his own with minimal effort.

Jason leaned back and explained, " You know, bulletin boards. It's what people used modems for before the internet came along. You would directly dial a number instead of logging onto the net, and it would hook you up to a kind of website hosted on somebody's home computer."

"So, you were basically just dialing people's houses?"

"Right. That's pretty much how it worked." Jason finished his beer, and Alex tried to polish his off at the same time in order to keep up with him. Jason met Alex's efforts with a look of near pity.

Alex caught the look on his roommate's face. "I'm not challenging you. I'm just trying to catch a buzz."

Jason relaxed and sat his empty can down beside his keyboard. "OK. Cause let's remember what happened the last time you challenged me."

"Let's not," said Alex. Of course, in that instant, he recalled exactly what had happened. He had gotten so drunk at a pizza joint near the college that Jason and the girls had to help him walk out of the place. Karen and Theresa were somewhat embarrassed but equally amused, and Jason had never let him hear the end of it. So much for drinking cheap beer by the pitcher. "So, what's so great about this bulletin board list?"

"Nothing really, but I found something strange. Look." Jason pointed to an item on the list.

Alex leaned forward to read it on the monitor. "The Inner Compendium. What's that?"

Jason could only shrug in response. "I'm not sure. I dialed it up on my modem, and it connected. All I saw was a blank screen with a cursor in the upper left corner. Then, it was like somebody slowly started typing on the other end." Jason moved his finger slowly across the screen to indicate how the text had appeared letter by letter. "Welcome to the Inner Compendium..."

"Dude, that is weird. Then what happened?"

Jason shook his head and reflected for a moment. "Nothing. Until this morning. I've been receiving these crazy e-mails all day with nothing but pictures of the woods and old cabins. And they're coming from that inner compendium group, but I can't trace it back to anyone because the messages don't contain a viable return e-mail address."

"Then how do you know that's where they're coming from?" Alex was growing all the more intrigued and certainly a bit creeped out by the whole thing.

"Listen to this. It's the first one that came in," said Jason with a gleam in his eyes and a somewhat disturbed look on his face. Jason opened his inbox and pulled up an e-mail. As he did so, a booming voice spoke over the computer's speakers.

"Welcome to the inner Compendium."

A Picture of a cabin in the woods was then loaded into the email message. Unbeknownst to either of them, it was the same cabin where Vanessa was murdered.

CHAPTER 4

Laura's hair fell softly across her shoulders as she unwrapped the towel from her head after taking a nice, long soak in the bathtub. She extinguished the flames from an assortment of candles in the bathroom and proceeded to light a few candles beside her bed, eager for a period of continued serenity before succumbing to the charms of sleep.

Selecting a digital track on a laptop sitting on the end table beside her bed, she crossed her legs, rested her hands on her knees, and began a controlled breathing pattern and recited a series of numbers in her mind. Meditation had become an almost nightly part of her life's routine. It not only provided her with a sense of calm, it often offered insights into her past and possibly her future. With her back pressed against the headboard, she sought those insights again.

Even as Laura was relaxing into a meditative state as part of her nightly bedtime ritual, Karen was lying down for the night in her dorm room. She was alone for the moment, Theresa having opted to stay at the library until a ghastly hour studying for an exam. Sleep came quickly, as Karen was mentally and physically exhausted from her own cramming sessions over the prior week. It did not, however, come gently. Karen soon began to exhibit signs of restlessness, writhing in the bed and moaning on occasion, the results of uncomfortable dreams that began to invade her mind as soon as she drifted off to sleep.

In her dreams, Karen found herself standing in a bathroom in an academic building on campus. It was nighttime, a faint trace of moonlight making its way into the women's room through windows near the sinks. While washing her hands, she began to sense something unwelcome in the room with her. Her heart began to beat in a nervous rhythm,

and her head filled with fog, as if the flow of time was somehow being altered. She didn't want to look around, to find the thing that stalked her....
Keeping her eyes down, she walked out of the bathroom into the hall beyond....

In the back of her mind, an image flashed. An image of a person with a boar's head staring over one of the stalls at her as she exited the bathroom, a grotesque fusion of human and swine with scars and piercing eyes....

Karen walked down the hallway, beginning to see out of the corner of her eye that she was being watched through the doors of classrooms and to feel that she was being followed. She kept her head down, a look of terror building on her face. As she reached the end of the hall and grabbed for the door to the outside, the boar man and three other creatures began chasing her. They shrieked and roared as they ran toward her, one with a wolf's head, another with a bear's head, and still another with the head of a giant carrion bird.

They followed her closely as she ran out of the building onto the campus grounds. She didn't even try to scream. She only thought of running. She only thought of evading her pursuers for a sufficient length of time as to find help from someone else at the college, someone else still awake at whatever hour of night it might be.

Following some undefined and unexpected instinct, she looked back over her shoulder and, for the moment, saw that her pursuers had seemingly vanished. Slowing, she turned back around and saw Theresa lying in a nearby fountain, bloodied and apparently dead. Her eyes were staring toward the night sky with no sign of consciousness dwelling behind them. Then the animal people were on her again. She ran even faster, only narrowly avoiding the outstretched claws of the boar person as she left Theresa at the fountain.

Passing the stairs to another class building at breakneck speed, Karen was horrified to see Alex and Jason chained to the stair rails. They had been beaten badly, and two cloaked, hooded figures were driving steel pins into them with hammers. They screamed in utter agony as she ran past, still desperate to escape the nightmare that had erupted all around her beloved campus home.

Finally, she arrived at the edge of a wooded area adjacent to the campus only to witness Laura sitting at the base of a tree, casually meditating as if nothing out of the ordinary was taking place around her.

Karen screamed, "Laura! Help me! Why won't you help me?"

Laura's eyes opened in a blank stare. She looked forward as if not even seeing Karen or any of her pursuers.

At that instant, Karen jerked into consciousness, leaving behind the nightmare. She sat up straight in bed, covered in sweat and breathing heavily. Her mind could scarcely process what would have led to such a nightmare. How could she even fear that Laura wouldn't be there for her if there was any sort of danger? She wiped her forehead and stretched back out on the bed, groaning from the frustration of having a bad dream when she was so exhausted from exam week.

CHAPTER 5

Late the following morning, after Theresa's last exam, the intrepid group of college students and their somewhat hesitant companion Laura gathered around Jason's van in the parking lot behind the dorm that housed mostly junior boys. Laura, Karen, and Theresa loaded their luggage and other provisions into the back of the vehicle and were surprised to see that it was actually quite a nice van and well-kept. There was the vague scent of work out gear that had perhaps been left in the back seat for too long on occasion, but other than that, it appeared they were in for a reasonably comfortable ride up to the heights of the nearby mountains. Jason and Alex were already sitting in the front of the van, having loaded their supplies and duffel bags before the ladies arrived.

Laura noted some signs of fatigue on Karen's face and in the way she carried herself.

"Are you alright? You don't look so good."

Karen brushed off any concern. "I had some nasty dreams last night. I couldn't go back to sleep. Are you ready for this?"

Laura grinned as she thought to herself that she wasn't sure she was ready at all. "Don't I look ready enough?" Laura held up a backpack and an overly large suitcase, which Theresa and Karen helped her squeeze into the storage area.

Jason then stuck his head out of the driver's side window and yelled, "Come on, ladies. Let's go!" Inside the van, he followed his shout with a dismissive statement to Alex, "You know this is a big pile of crap, don't you?"

Alex was accustomed to his friend and roommate's blunt nature and knew exactly what he was referencing, but he wanted to hear Jason say it. "What precisely is a big pile of crap?"

Jason immediately retorted, "This paranormal, ghost-hunting thing you and those chicks have cooked up. It's moronic. What you see is what you get. That's all there is. That's why I'm into technology. It's real, not a figment of peoples' imaginations."

Alex responded without any hint of harshness in his tone,"So why did you decide to come then?"

"To find new places to drink beer all night and sleep till noon."

"It's good to have a goal," said Alex. He didn't disagree with the general sentiment of Jason's goal, but he was completely on board with the paranormal investigation that his friend was rejecting. It had been a growing interest of his since middle school. He thought of those days and how his friendship with Jason had begun long before college, back in the elementary school years.

In eighth grade, Alex had been given a devil of a time by a bully who was pretty much too big to be in a biker gang, much less middle school. He was six feet and two inches tall and built like a brick crapper or at least a relatively dumpy crapper at the whopping age of fourteen. He was a straight up redneck who made no effort to be anything else, and he tormented Alex on a daily basis. Most of the teachers were afraid of the guy. One day when he was bugging Alex to the point that he couldn't get a moment's peace, Jason stepped in and told him to back off and leave Alex alone. That was all it took to break the cycle of bullying. Thinking of that moment, Alex was suddenly very glad his friend was coming along on this trip. After all, the mountainside might be populated with who knows what creepy assholes. He could take care of himself now in a way that he obviously couldn't in middle school, but it didn't hurt to have Jason nearby in a pinch. As the ladies piled in and Jason fired the van up, Alex felt free and a bit euphoric. It was going to be a fun trip... one to remember.

* * *

Later that afternoon, they arrived at a clearing on the outskirts of a small town in the mountains called Stinton's Lure. They stopped to set up camp for the night, not because they couldn't reach Maggie View before the day was out, but simply because they wanted to spend a night camping before they moved on. The clearing was just a couple of hours away from the college, or at least that's what it took on the meandering back highways between Cullowdale and Maggie View.

Still nestled in the foothills with the mountains beginning to rise steeply around them, they unloaded some necessary supplies out of the van and set up camp around a small fire. The ladies relaxed and engaged in civilized conversation near the fire while Alex and Jason started in on a case of cheap beer while sitting near the tents.

With a glint in her eye that indicated she had fond memories of her own college days, Laura glanced over at the guys and their drinking activities. "Please tell me that's not all they ever do."

Karen responded, "Don't worry. They'll drink themselves sick the first couple of days, then put it down for a week or so till they forget how sick they got."

Theresa began to dig around for something in her backpack. "I think there may be a more civilized way for us to relax and still wake up feeling quite refreshed and feminine in the morning."

"Do tell," said Karen.

Theresa pulled a bottle of white wine out of her backpack and held it up for their inspection.

"I'm up for that," Laura said while digging a few disposable plastic cups out of her own luggage.

Theresa worked to open the bottle with a corkscrew she also found in her backpack while Karen sat with a look of considerable eagerness on her face. "This is good stuff. I've had it before. Theresa's parents run a family vineyard."

"Really, Theresa? I didn't know that," asked Laura.

"Sure do. They bottle the best Chard you'll ever taste. I'm planning to carry on the tradition. If I manage to, I'll be the third generation to do so."

Laura felt proud of her young companion. "That's great. I hope it works out. So, what's on the agenda for tomorrow? Is there an agenda?"

Karen answered, "Tomorrow, we go into town for a local ghost tour. I've been on it before. It's really good. Should provide some inspiration anyway."

By this point, Theresa had the bottle open and poured a glass for Laura first.

Laura raised her cup in an imperious but grateful fashion, "To ghosts!"

Her companions responded in kind, "To ghosts!"

* * *

Later that night, they all gathered around the campfire, the lads having decided to play some part in the genteel conversation. By that point, however, Jason and Alex both were on the verge of passing out and had little to contribute to the discussion.

Karen offered some free advice. "Look at them. Why don't you guys just go to sleep already?"

"Soon enough," Jason said.

"Sure, Mommy," chimed Alex.

Karen gave them a look that would melt steel. "Oh, watch it."

Theresa drove the conversation in a more somber direction as she looked at Laura with an inquisitive and somewhat serious look on her face. "So, what did you see before?"

Laura didn't quite get what she was referring to at first and asked, "Before?"

"You know. When you went ghost hunting," Theresa continued.

Laura paused for just a second, just long enough to give the impression that she was offering a response that she had spoken before or had thought through before, "Oh. It was weird. We weren't supposed to be ghost-hunting. We were staying at a little cabin for the weekend, and I had stepped outside to get away from the cigarette smoke for awhile. When I came back in, I saw my friends sitting in a circle on the floor doing some sort of made-up seance. I started to laugh at them before I could even get through the door because I knew they were just drunk and being stupid...." Laura paused again, a bit longer this time. "Then we all saw it, just as I walked through the door. A spectral figure. It appeared in the air for just a second, and then it was gone."

"What did it look like," Theresa asked, her eyes now wide upon hearing Laura's recounting of the experience.

"Just this flash of light in the air, kind of

human shaped from what we saw of it."

Jason piped up with a bit of a slur in his speech, the clear result of consuming a considerable number of beers over the afternoon and evening, "Ever heard of headlights?"

Alex immediately took exception to the remark. "How could a headlight have done that?"

"I don't know. Reflected somehow, off of something.... I would have to know more about the conditions..."

Laura responded with certainty. "No. It wasn't headlights. There were no cars around. Anyway, sweet dreams, everybody." She added the last bit, thinking that she just might have scared some of them a little and that a touch of humor might be in order.

"Don't worry. I'm gonna sleep just fine," said Jason. He then immediately stumbled to his tent, climbed in, passed out, and began snoring within a minute.

The others just looked on and chuckled, then managed to shift the conversation away from ghosts before they called it a night as well.

* * *

That night, shortly after the midnight hour, Laura began to have night dreams that seemed as real to her as any waking moment.

She saw Jarret sitting in the same back room of the old country store, the room that had been among the last things her mother had seen on Earth.

He spoke to her, "I was the one who hid you from the dark seekers, Laura."

She then saw three men and four women dressed in dark robes, their faces covered by cowls. They moved into the room and walked over to surround Jarret. Then a large man dressed all in black with a hood covering his entire head entered. He had large biceps and carried an ax. They all seemed to be oblivious to her presence, as if she were invisible and Jarret's words to her couldn't be heard by them.

Jarret continued, "I paid the ultimate price for it, but I knew you must be protected from the darkness that wanted to claim you."

One of the women advanced toward Jarret, pulling back her hood to reveal her face. She was an older woman, brandishing a terrifying scowl.

Jarret looked her directly in the face, showing no signs of being intimidated by her. "You are fear, but you don't scare me."

"Where is the girl?" asked the woman with a craggy voice like that of a dark witch from some other world.

Jarret ignored the woman and spoke once again to Laura. "Soon, you will no longer be able to hide from your past. Something dark has found you."

The man with the ax raised it high in the air as if preparing to swing it down at Jarret. Laura woke from the dream without so much as a start and stared up at the sky.

* * *

The next morning, Alex, Theresa, and Laura were busily cleaning up the camp site and loading their luggage into the van when Jason sat up in his sleeping bag, wiped his eyes, and groaned. Looking over at Alex, he asked, "What time is it, man?"

"About ten o'clock."

"Throw me a beer."

Alex propped open the lid of a cooler and pulled a warm beer out of the largely melted ice in the bottom. He tossed it over to Jason. Jason immediately popped the can open and began to drink.

"Mmm. Breakfast of champeens," Jason practically sang.

"I can't believe you," Theresa said.

Karen emerged from the womens' tent dressed in jogging pants and a tee shirt. She looked down at Jason as he drank a beer before so much as climbing out of his sleeping bag.

"Pitiful." With that, she ran off into the woods, following a clearly defined trail.

Jason yelled after her, "They've proven alcohol is good for you, you know!"

The others chuckled and shrugged as they continued with the work of packing up the campsite and dousing the remnants of the fire.

"What? I do work out, in case you haven't noticed. I bet I'm in better shape than her."

"Sure, Jason. Just keep telling yourself that," said Theresa.

"Come on. Get up and help us," commanded Laura.

Jason drained the rest of his beer as he slowly got out of the sleeping bag and managed to stand up.

"I'm helping. I'm tons of help."

Not so far away, Karen was running along the trail, just beginning to work up a good sweat. Suddenly, the wind kicked up around her. She stopped to look around, trying to determine what could possibly cause such a localized gust of wind that seemed to effectively be centered on her. Confused, she brushed off some debris and kept running.

* * *

A short time later, Alex and the others had nearly finished cleaning up the camp site. Jason was taking down the women's tent.

Alex piped up as if forgetting the presence of the ladies, "I'm gonna go drain the lizard."

Theresa cringed and turned to Alex. "Oh, thanks for letting us in on that, Alex. You're such a dork." She turned back to Laura and exchanged a knowing look that implied, "Boys are just stupid."

Jason missed the look that passed between them but offered his own advice to his intrepid roommate, "Watch out for mosquitoes."

Laura followed up with, "And snakes."

Theresa whispered as Alex walked off, waving bye to them without further comment. "Was that supposed to be Freudian?"

"You tell me."

"You girls are pervs," Jason said. "You need to quit ragging on me about being bad... or immature... or whatever you routinely say...."

"You just need to not have such good hearing," replied Theresa while returning to her work.

"I'll do my best, but I wouldn't count on it. Just wash your mouth out with soap, and it won't be a problem."

* * *

A couple of minutes later, Alex was standing in the woods, zipping up his pants after relieving himself, when an utterly unexpected sound made its way to his ears. As if carried on the wind in the tone of a harsh whisper, he heard a man's voice say, "You first!"

Alex looked around in shock. He could see nothing, no people, no animals, only trees and foliage. A second time, "You first!"

This time, Alex heard someone approaching. Laura stepped into sight after a moment on the trail that led him to this spot in the woods.

"Oh, I'm sorry, Alex. I'm not following you. I promise."

"That's OK. I'm done. You didn't see anybody around here, did you?"

Laura seemed surprised by the question, "No. Like who?"

"I get the feeling Jason is trying to play a little trick on me."

"I wouldn't put it past him, but he was still at camp when I left. I'm not really sure how he could be playing tricks."

Alex shrugged off her response, "Anyway, That's my spot. I marked it well." He pointed to the ground a couple of feet in front of him.

"Um, sure. I'll try to avoid that area. Thanks for the warning." Laura rolled her eyes and continued walking along the path after that as Alex chuckled to himself and headed back for camp, intent on discovering exactly how the technologically savvy Jason had managed to prank him in the middle of the wilderness.

* * *

Having relieved herself in the woods a healthy fifty paces away from Alex's spot, Laura was beginning her own trek back to camp when she suddenly sensed a presence nearby.

She looked up to see a cloaked, hooded man in front of her. She stopped in her tracks and gasped but said nothing, weighing her options for an instant.

The man pulled an axe from behind his back and began to chase her. No longer considering options, she ran deeper into the woods with the man following close on her heels. As she ran, she noticed other cloaked and hooded figures sitting in high tree branches, silently watching the chase.

Just when Laura thought she had lost the man, he emerged from nowhere. Laura stopped, summoned all her resolve and spoke to him.

"Who are you? Why am I seeing you?"

At first, the man stood still as a headstone. Then he raised the axe high above his head as if he was about to swing it at her. Laura raised her arm in defense and closed her eyes. Nothing happened.

After a terrifying moment, she opened

her eyes and saw nothing.

CHAPTER 6

Laura helped the others finish loading their camping gear back into the van and climbed into the front passenger seat for a better view as they traversed the narrow mountain highway leading the remainder of the way to Maggie View. Maggie was an extraordinarily quaint town nestled in the foothills at the outer edge of an extensive and minimally populated mountain range. As they cruised along with the windows down, reveling in the mountain breeze like hippies on a quest for self-discovery, Laura found herself amused by the banter between Alex and Jason. Alex was convinced that Jason had played some kind of trick on him in the woods. Jason responded that Alex was already in a highly suggestible state of mind and that he would be dreaming up ghosts before they even arrived at their destination. From there, the conversation descended into a debate over exactly how Jason was supposed to have pranked him. Alex suggested the use of some kind of transmitters, which Jason found sublimely laughable. They were all still goading the debate and teasing Alex for his lack of technical knowledge as they passed the welcome sign for the town of Maggie View.

Upon their arrival, Alex and Jason joined Theresa in the search for some final additions to their supplies while Karen and Laura took advantage of the opportunity to sit down and enjoy a coffee at the Giant Spoon Cafe. Laura favored a latte with hints of cinnamon and chocolate, while Karen selected a mocha blend topped off with a layer of whipped cream.

"Mmm. This is good coffee," Karen gently moaned as they sat looking out at the town's tiny main street.

"Yeah, I needed this," said Laura, her thoughts drifting in the direction of the tranquility afforded by Maggie View's isolation and quaint features.

Karen interrupted Laura's thoughts, "So, did you come through Maggie View on the trip you took in college?"

Laura took her by surprise, "More than that. I grew up around here."

"You're kidding me. I thought you came from up north or something. You mean you actually grew up in this town?"

"No, about an hour south of here, but I was born in this town and lived here a few months till I got adopted by a couple from Hickory. By the time I was twelve, we were moving around all over the place. I guess that's why I have a neutral accent."

Karen was all the more taken aback. "I didn't know you were adopted either."

Laura nonchalantly responded, "You learn something new every day, right?"

"Do you know your biological parents? I mean, if you don't mind me asking. I don't want to bring up a sore subject."

"Unfortunately, no. My mother was killed when I was an infant. I don't know anything about my father except that he had already left her."

"I'm sorry. I didn't know," blushed Karen, as she looked down at her coffee and away from Laura.

"Don't worry about it. I never really knew either one of them."

The two of them lapsed back into silence for a moment, staring out at the small town beyond the cafe's windows. Karen tried to think of something to steer the conversation in a different direction and break the silence but failed to do so. Fortunately, Laura broke through the slightly awkward pause and rescued their discussion.

"Yeah. There's nothing like a decadent hot drink, summer or no... To me, there is no more wonderful thing than time to sit and sip... I could pretty much do this every waking moment..."

"Of course," said Karen. "I mean, looking for ghosts is a cozy affair, right? To be undertaken with a belly full of luscious, warm beverages."

After that, they sat and sipped until they were forced to depart from the cafe in order to meet their companions at the appointed time for the local ghost walk.

* * *

As dusk approached, bringing with it the chirping of crickets from the town's abundant verdure, Laura and the others stood amidst a small group of tourists gathered around the two guides of the local ghost walk. The guides were lifetime residents of Maggie View, Anna and Elise. Anna and her partner in the paranormal, both wrapped in long black cloaks despite the warmth of the summer evening, looked out upon their audience and raised their vintage lamps high for all to see. Anna was a tall, thin woman in her forties with a long nose and unkempt sandy hair. She apparently had an affection for over-sized, 1980s-style glasses, or she was simply wearing a pair she had somehow managed to hang on to since the 80s. Elise was a plain-looking woman in her thirties with short-cropped brunette hair and a choker necklace that stood out for its fusion of gold and black stones and gems.

Anna started the festivities as she addressed the crowd, "Greetings to all and welcome to our tour of the supernatural."

Continuing the theme, Elise joined in, "Tonight, you will join us on a journey through the history of some of the bloodiest events that have ever occurred in our town... and the resulting discontented spirits that still haunt some of the beautiful homes that line our downtown streets."

"If you're faint of heart, don't worry, we have a good reputation for bringing everyone back alive... as a general rule," said Anna.

Elise grinned. "Everyone follow me, and my esteemed colleague will bring up the rear."

The crowd began to walk behind Elise as Alex and Theresa moved toward the rear of the group to speak with Anna.

Alex asked her, "Have you ever actually seen a ghost?"

"Sure I have."

Theresa's excitement grew. "On the tour?"

"We think we got a little glimpse of a spook once, but I got a lot better look than that when I was by myself one night."

"Cool," Theresa responded.

Anna snickered at Theresa's enthusiasm as the group moved down the sidewalk past several street front businesses and onto a street lined with homes built between the mid-1800s and early 1900s.

Anna stopped the group in front of a Colonial home that had been renovated and kept in extraordinarily good condition. It was white with black shutters and a lovely flower garden in the small front yard.

Anna began her first tale of the evening. "This is the Stanton house. It's over a hundred and fifty years old, and it remains one of the finer homes in town. It has undergone three renovations within the last century. She paused dramatically. It is also home to the most brutal ghost story to be heard in these parts. In the 1920s, the last generation of Stantons to own this home were all wiped out in a single night. You see, Daryl Stanton went out of his head one night and chopped up his family with an old Civil War sword. No one has ever sufficiently explained what drove him to do this. He just came home from a meeting in town one evening and went berserk, killing his wife, son, and daughter. Then, the sheriff shot Daryl right there on the front porch. Anna paused again for effect. It's been said by many residents of this home down through the years that you can often hear the horrible sounds of that night's slaughter echoing through the house, climaxing with a gunshot and a man's final moans of agony.

"This house is also unique in that one of the ghosts that haunts its aged halls has occasionally been known to attack the living. One night, amidst all the ghostly noises, a heavy ashtray flew across the room and struck a man in the head, nearly killing him."

Once again, Elise began to lead the group down the street as the tourists spoke softly among themselves.

Alex looked at Jason. "What do you think now?"Jason shrugged and seemed unimpressed. Alex knew that it was going to require more than stories to get Jason to believe in what he couldn't necessarily see, record, and analyze.

The next house the group came to was a brightly colored Victorian home adorned with pinkish hues, and white window shutters dappled with gray dots. Elise paused near a gate in the fence that surrounded the house and began to tell her own ghost story in a dramatic voice that instantly carried chills across her audience.

"The tale of the Ludlow house is one of the gentler stories you'll hear tonight. This is actually a case of a friendly ghost. They call her Stacy. She is the ghost of a former resident who died in the house of old age. No one is really sure why she remains, but most people feel it is because she had a good life here and loves the house. If it ain't broke, don't fix it, I guess."

The crowd chuckled at this and seemed to embrace a moment of levity. Elise reveled in the laughter for just a moment and then continued, "Stacy appears with great frequency, and it is said that about twenty to thirty years ago, she was joined by another female ghost who appears on rare occasions. Nothing is known about this ghost, only that she has been seen in the same house and that she has a mischievous tendency to move objects around or make them disappear altogether, particularly nick knacks and jewelry. So, everyone, keep an eye on your family jewels...."

There was another round of chuckles as Anna led everyone away from the lovely Victorian house. "Now, if everyone will follow me, we have one more house to visit, and then we will call it a night so that the living can get some dinner."

After visiting the final house of the tour, Laura and the others gathered near Anna and Elise, hoping to ask a few questions after the other tourists moved along.

Anna noticed they were lingering, "So, what did you guys think?"

"It was great," Theresa said.

Alex agreed, "Yeah, we loved it."

Karen felt the need to point out something more specific, feeling that the truncated responses of her friends might come across as disingenuous, "Especially the house with the friendly ghost. I like friendly ghosts."

Elise seemed pleased with their enthusiasm, "In that case, you all should come by later. We're having a cookout there."

"You should spend the night there if you

like friendly ghosts. You just might see one," challenged Anna.

Laura laughed. "I don't know how the owners would feel about that."

Anna and Elise exchanged amused looks.

"I do. I am the owner," Anna said. "You guys are welcome to stay tonight, no charge. I get the feeling you came here looking for more than a casual ghost tour."

Jason smirked. "Whatever gave you that idea? These guys only asked more questions than a little kid riding a sugar high."

Karen accepted the invitation for the group, "Definitely. We should stay." She then looked to the others, and they nodded in agreement.

With that, Jason and Alex left to reacquire the van from the parking space they had found for it earlier in the afternoon. Laura and the others joined Anna and Elise on their way back home.

* * *

An hour later, they all stood in the back yard of Anna and Elise's lovely home, sipping on a few freshly mixed drinks and enjoying the pair's generosity in the form of grilled chicken and burgers.

Karen stood with a tall glass full of a pink concoction that was clearly satisfying her desire for sweets. "Mmm. This is good. Anna mixes a great Shirley Temple."

Theresa gave a knowing look to Elise. "She's the temperate one of the group."

Laura seemed surprised she wasn't being thrown into the temperate category as the post-college senior member of their little party. "What about me? I'm pretty temperate. Right?"

"Sorry, you too," Theresa responded, amused that Laura seemed concerned with the designation.

Elise changed the subject, eager to delve into the group's interest in the paranormal. "How goes the ghost hunting so far? Seen anything?"

"No, and I'm afraid with our total lack of sophisticated equipment, we won't be detecting anything at all," said Theresa.

"I bet we do in the mountains," Laura interjected.

Elise seemed suddenly concerned, her

face furrowing a bit. "What mountains? I mean, what area of the mountains specifically?"

Karen replied in a nonchalant fashion, "We're headed up to Miller's Ridge tomorrow."

"For how long?" asked Elise, her concern clearly growing from the tone of her voice and the look on her face.

"Several nights. We rented a cabin," said Theresa.

Elise issued a friendly admonition, "I'd be careful up there if I were you. People go missing sometimes. And this isn't tour guide talk either. I'm serious as a heart attack."

Theresa was suddenly developing her own concerns, "Is there someone up there who doesn't like outsiders or something?"

"I don't know," Elise answered, "Your guess is as good as mine, but something ain't right up there."

Laura spoke with confidence, clearly trying to sooth everyone's nerves, "We'll stick together. I'm sure we'll be alright."

After that, Elise backed off her warnings, feeling she had done her duty. The conversation about the town's history and its eccentricities went on for some time, and they all called it a night with full bellies and a shared sensation that they just might find something interesting in the nearby mountains.

* * *

That night, in the parlor of Anna and Elise's house, Laura sat up, lost in thought, as Karen and Theresa slept soundly on nearby sofas. She saw that the boys had nodded off in their sleeping bags atop a plush rug in the center of the room. One of them was gently snoring. Laura couldn't determine with certainty who it was as she sat staring at a bracelet that she and Theresa had noticed sitting on an end table earlier in the evening. Laura had thought there was something familiar about it, as if it had belonged to someone she knew many years before.

Laura didn't so much as stir in her seat as the bracelet slowly moved across the table top, dropped to the floor, and moved along the floor in her direction, guided by some unseen hand or force.

She watched calmly, and when the bracelet brushed against her foot, she reached down to pick it up. She put the bracelet on her wrist and looked into the air around her.

Laura whispered, "You're not Stacy, are you now?" She looked back at the bracelet and touched it with her opposite hand. "No, I thought not."

With that, she picked up a half-full glass of wine and drained it, then leaned her head back and closed her eyes. "Do you have the answers, dear friendly spirit?"

* * *

Even as Laura and the others were calling it a night in the quaint Victorian home of their new friends in Maggie View, a young couple marched through the woods near Miller's Ridge with minimal camping gear on their backs. High on the mountainside, Darren and Cindy walked close together, carrying camping lamps to light their way through the woods. They stopped for a moment to get their bearings, and as the light from his lamp fell on Cindy's curvy body and blonde mop of hair, Darren's thoughts began to follow an entirely sensual path. What he didn't realize was that Cindy was looking back at him in the beam of her own lamp, annoyed at his seeming lack of a sense of direction but entirely open to the same kind of thinking... or acting... as she was reminded of his piercing blue eyes and jet black hair.

Cindy allowed her annoyance to take precedence over her hormones, "Are you sure you remember where this spot is?"

Darren responded enthusiastically, "Absolutely. It's unforgettable." He then stepped up and grabbed her backside with both hands. "Just like you. Why don't I just chase you there!"

Cindy laughed and pulled away. She began to run, and Darren chased her.

As Darren drew close to catching her, they suddenly found themselves in a clearing in which stood an old log cabin. A narrow dirt road led away from the cabin, down the side of the mountain. They stopped in surprise. Unbeknownst to them, the cabin was the same one that appeared on the monitor in Jason's room earlier... the same one by which Vanessa met her untimely end many years before.

Cindy noticed the dirt road leading away from the cabin and put her hands on her hips.

"Why didn't we just follow the road up here?"

"That wouldn't have been any fun," Darren quipped.

"Oh, I can't believe you, Darren Travers. Here I was, thinking we were lost in the woods for good. I was scared!"

Darren moved close and put his arms around her, kissing her gently. "What's to be scared of out here?"

They both looked up then and realized to their terror that they were surrounded by the figures from Laura's dreams. The members of the compendium all removed their hoods, revealing men and women of various ages. Some of their faces were covered in burns and odd scars. Others were free of these marks.

Darren and Cindy had nowhere to flee.

CHAPTER 7

The following morning, Laura and her young companions said farewell to their gracious hosts and departed Maggie View for the heights of the surrounding mountains. They wound their way up meandering back roads that led away from the quaint town, feeling instantly as if they were entering another world, a world in which life was driven less by daily work and school routines or social media obsessions.

From the driver's seat, Jason piped up, "Somebody toss me a beer."

"Uh, no beer for the driver. That's a rule," Karen responded.

Theresa couldn't repress a laugh, "Your love of nature knows no limits, does it, Jason? I mean, toss me a beer before I start hugging trees or something...."

"It's just my love of suds that knows no limits. I have no problem with trees and grass as a backdrop for drinking it."

Laura thought of her own college days and forgave the beer-driven conversation. She did, however, steer the discussion in another direction. "Have any of you guys seen this cabin you rented?"

Jason responded, "No. Alex is the only one who's even been up on Miller's Ridge before, right?"

"Yeah, I camped there once. It's first class all the way this time, though. Laura, Karen says you were born around here. Didn't you ever come up to the ridge?"

Laura responded in a nonchalant fashion, "No. I'm sorry to say I missed out on that."

She knew this wasn't true, but she wasn't ready to share anything more of her background with the group. They had asked her to come along. She wasn't obligated to tell them of whatever ties her family may have had to the area. After all, she was reasonably sure there was no real danger despite what she suspected of her family's past. Or, so she told herself.

* * *

A few minutes later, as the road began to arch upward at a steep angle, Jason pulled the van over at a small country store, the same store that once played host to conversations between Jarrett and others in the back room.

As Jason parked the van near the shabby store, Laura looked up and inquired, "What are we doing here?"

"We have to pick up the keys to the cabin," responded Alex as they all began to climb out of the van. "And we might as well take one last pass at supplies while we can because there is nothing from here on up – absolutely nothing but stray cabins here and there and probably a ranger station somewhere, but who knows?"

After they entered the store, the owner emerged from the back office to present Alex and Jason with the keys and directions to the cabin. As they talked, Laura walked through the store and took a moment to glance into the back room. The same cultural and religious icons remained in place as they had been in Jarret's day, still resting on table tops and hanging on the walls. Laura had been here before but was unaware of exactly what the connection was between the store and her past. She could sense some trace of her mother's past in the store. That's all she was certain of.

Karen approached her. "Want something to drink?"

Laura brought herself back to the present, "I'd love a water. Thanks."

"Are you OK? You seem a little distracted," queried Karen.

"Yeah. I'm fine. I guess I just didn't sleep very well last night," Laura lied and once again lost herself in troubled thoughts of her enigmatic family history.

CHAPTER 8

Laura and the others arrived at the cabin a
short time later, the summer sun beating down
on them. They exited the van, immediately
beginning to sweat profusely as they carried
supplies and luggage in the direction of the
front door. The cabin was the same one at
which Darren and Cindy had experienced
their harrowing encounter with the mysterious
group the night before. It was also the same
cabin at which Laura's mother had died and the
very cabin that had played host to paranormal
experiences for Laura on more than one occasion
in the past. She saw no danger in the place, being
unaware of the nature of her mother's demise,
but she revealed nothing of her familiarity with

it to her enthusiastic friends.

Alex, however, noticed something that sent a chill up his spine. He pulled Jason aside and whispered, "Dude. You see it, don't you?"

"What?"

"You don't see it?"

"See what, man? What am I supposed to be seeing?"

"This is the cabin from those photos that crazy bulletin board sent you," Alex said, his face and tone revealing obvious concern.

Jason shrugged, "No, it isn't. You're imagining things again, just like that voice you thought you heard in the woods. I mean, I admit it looks a little like it, but it's a cabin. They all look alike."

"I don't know, man."

"I do. It can't be the same one," Jason assured him and quickly grabbed another piece of luggage, intent on getting out of the heat for a while.

"I hope you're right," Alex said, following him and trying to get a grip on himself before any of the others noticed he was scared.

Jason laughed, "Come on, you big baby.

We've got beer to drink and a log toilet to break in."

Theresa crossed paths with them just in time to overhear this pronouncement from Jason, "Charming Jason. Truly charming."

* * *

The cabin was old but had been relatively well maintained over the years. The ground floor consisted of one great room with a kitchen at the back, partially separated from the rest of the floor by a bar with a row of cabinets situated above it. There was a large dining table on one side of the room and a couple of couches and end tables on the other side of the room, positioned close to a fire place. There were two bedrooms upstairs with some single beds randomly strewn about, and there was one bathroom between the two bedrooms. All in all, it was rustic but functional, offering running water, a full kitchen, and electricity provided by a gas generator behind the cabin.

As the sun set, Alex and Theresa began preparing a dinner for the five of them. Laura made her way down the stairs after a brief nap. She stepped in for a quick peek at what they were cooking, and she wondered if there would be a need before this trip was over to enlighten her friends with her true knowledge of the ridge and even the very cabin in which they were to be sleeping.

Theresa was leaning over a skillet full of sizzling chicken, stirring it around with a spatula. "Oh, this chicken is going to be so good. Grab the tarragon for me, would you?"

Alex complied, "Only you would bring fine herbs and spices on a road trip like this. But it's endearing though, really it is."

Theresa cracked a smile. "Thanks. Now hand me the tarragon."

"Smells delicious," said Laura as she backed out of the kitchen and strolled over to join Karen and Jason in the den.

Karen was spreading out a deck of cards on a coffee table near the couches. "Come on. We have time for a couple of quick hands before dinner. Although, you know I'm gonna win. Nobody beats me at cards."

"Why are we even playing then?" asked Laura.

Karen replied in a curt but logical fashion,

"Well, it's fun for me."

"Oh, I see. I wouldn't want to be the one to put an end to your fun," Laura said as she crossed her legs and waited on Karen to deal.

At the dining table, Jason attached a pair of small speakers to his Tablet. With a look on his face that indicated he was quite proud of himself, he clicked a couple of buttons, and a song was heard throughout the great room.

"Is that sound amazing or what?" crowed Jason. "It's like I have a giant boom box, but look at the size of these little speakers!" With that, Jason began to dance badly.

On the other side of the room, Laura and Karen could only scoff and exchange a knowing look.

"Yeah, that's great, Jason. Your day's work is done," Karen spouted as she turned her attention quickly back to the cards.

"Nice, Jason," Laura said, as she began to sift through the hand Karen had dealt her. "I think it indicates some commendable self-actualization on your part that you are willing to do something so awkward in front of others."

"Huh?" responded Jason, not slowing in

his efforts to dance.

Theresa broke into the conversation as she called out from the kitchen, "Just remember we're having dinner on that table in about twenty minutes."

At that, Jason stopped dancing and sat down at the table in front of his tablet, "Nobody appreciates me. That's OK. I don't need appreciation."

* * *

After a dinner of chicken in a lemon cream sauce with rice pilaf and chocolate drizzled pecan pie for desert, neither Laura nor her friends were in the mood to stake out wayward spirits in an isolated cabin on the side of a mountain. Things had been slightly too luxurious to that point to set the proper mood. Jason, Karen, and Laura casually cleared the table after dinner while Alex and Theresa took a much-deserved rest on the couches in the den.

"You know, I'd like to start a fire for ambiance," Alex said, "but it just isn't cold in here at all."

Alex kicked back with his feet on a nearby coffee table, listening to the pleasant clanking of post-dinner clatter and nothing more.

Suddenly, the silence was broken by the sound of Jason's tablet coming to life. The dark and somber voice of a man began to broadcast throughout the great room of the cabin – a voice no one could identify.

It was Jarret's voice... emerging from the past or growing into the present... lending a dangerous meaning to the words that none of them quite understood....

These non-recurring dreams,
all too profound in their single appearance
on the battle-bound landscape of my swaying
consciousness...

Karen started, "What is that?"

Jason strolled over, "I don't know. I guess I left my tablet on, but I don't know what it's playing."

Jarret's voice continued,

Just two or three of them that out flank the other
thousands,
like a giant's feet upon tainted ground,

like a few great mountains before the sea,
they speak of light, how vivid,
God sending visions to the high places.

Laura moved close to the speakers with a shocked look on her face. "It can't be...."

"What?" asked Jason.

"A poem. That was from a poem I wrote when I was in college."

Karen spoke up, trying to calm her own troubled nerves, "Oh, that can't be. Are you sure?"

"I'm sure. No one has ever read that poem... no one. It was from a private journal I used to keep. I go back and read through it once in a while."

"Guys, I don't like this. I don't like this at all," said Karen.

Alex was quick to walk over and offer some calming words, "Me either, but I'm sure someone is just playing a joke on us."

"Yeah, of course so," Jason said, "I don't know who could have found your poem, but somebody is playing a high-tech prank."

Theresa put her arm around Karen and

tried to convince herself that she believed the explanation Alex and Jason were offering. She wouldn't even put it past them to have pulled this prank themselves. That would be the easiest explanation, but she tried giving them the benefit of her doubts. "Half of Jason's fraternity knows he was going on this trip, and they would do anything to embarrass him about it."

Karen showed signs of relief on her face, but she was still on edge just thinking about the words that had invaded the cabin, "I guess you're right."

Laura piped up, "Maybe one of them broke into my office and found the journal. I think it's in the bottom of a drawer, somewhere."

Jason grinned, "See? Think rationally. There's no reason to get spooked. The DJ is just gonna crank some tunes and get rid of the mean, old poetry."

Everyone laughed and continued clearing the table, except for Jason. He went to the tablet and turned some music back on. As he did so, he noticed a message on the screen. "You have been visited by the Inner Compendium. Expect us again." Jason whispered to himself,

"I'm going to waste whoever is doing this."

CHAPTER 9

About an hour after dinner, Alex set about the work of mounting a digital camera on a tripod as Laura watched. She thought about the futility of applying such devices to the search for activity in the beyond. She knew it was there, could feel it... capturing some manifestation of it on a camera made no difference to her. But then, she never shared these feelings with anyone. "So what kind of ghosts are we expecting to see up on this mountain?" she asked, knowing Alex wouldn't have much of an answer.

Alex chucked, "To be honest, none. I just wanted to come up here. We probably won't be running into any spooks till we're back in another town on another ghost tour."

"Pity."

"I know," Alex responded as he finished with his work setting up the camera, "but then maybe not so much. Cold drinks and good conversation... no classes to make in the morning... those are better than ghost sightings anyway."

At that moment, Theresa and Karen made their way downstairs as Jason emerged from the kitchen with a couple of beers, tossing one to Alex.

"Should we really be filming them?" queried Karen. She was referring to Jason and Alex rather than any ghostly forms. She was mildly concerned about what kind of behavior they might capture on camera before the night was over.

Theresa answered with a question, "Why not?"

"OK. You make a compelling argument."

Alex selected some music on the tablet, a well chosen assortment of moody tunes from various seventies prog rock bands. The tunes fit the mood, although most of the group was unfamiliar with them. As the music played,

Karen and Theresa started a round of poker at the kitchen table. Jason and Alex drank their beers while reducing the light levels in the room to test the night vision on the camera. Laura sat on the sofa, her mind steadily invaded by a feeling of discomfort.

"Guys, we can't play poker in the dark," piped up Theresa.

"Make it a round of strip poker, and I will light this place up like daylight," Jason tried with a hint of a hopeful grin on his face.

"That's not happening," said Karen. "Get on with your testing, and give up on that line of thought."

"I just had to try, that's all."

A now familiar voice suddenly interrupted their conversation, overriding the outpouring of music from the tablet.

They all stopped in their tracks, unable to digest exactly what was happening.

Strange luminescence...
We could not find its source.
It beckoned, promising folds of night
to hide us from the wrecking wheel of the day.

"Oh, no. Not again," Karen whispered as she began to back as far away from the tablet as she could get.

The voice continued.

Odd tap on the glass....

They all heard a tapping sound but could see no cause for it....

It summoned us.
Into velvet wrappings, we proceeded,
only to discover the temporal nature of such veiled entrance.
Even now, I recall the morning's chill.

Theresa looked in Laura's direction, trying to remain calm and remind herself that surely they were being pranked, "One of yours this time?"

Laura had grown deadly serious, her countenance fully darkened by the events unfolding around her, "No. But somehow, I know what it means."

"What could it mean?" Alex asked.

"Someone is playing a joke, that's all... a good one, but a joke."

"Fear. That's what it means. We should be afraid," said Laura, the look on her face beginning to disturb everyone, with the exception of Jason.

Jason walked over to examine the tablet, "Look, again, just calm down, everybody. You're making yourselves afraid... for no good reason..."

At that moment, the front door of the old cabin burst open. They all turned in shock.

Instead of the fraternity pranksters that Jason and Alex half expected to see, the doorway was filled with the disturbing presence of a person they had never seen before.

Before them stood a muscular man over six feet tall, wearing ragged clothing and holding a large scimitar in one hand. There was evidence of strange scarring on his face and arms, scarring that had perhaps been inflicted upon him intentionally.

Even Jason took a step back in fear, and then they all entered that state of shock that only occurs in nightmares. For a moment, all of their bodies pulsed with such adrenaline they could neither speak nor move.

The odd sight before them seemed to shimmer for a moment, appearing insubstantial for just an instant, just long enough for them to realize that, in some sense, they had found what they came looking for.

Then the man was all too solid, entirely real and terrifying as he charged through the room toward them, blade raised and ready to strike.

Karen found her voice and, in her state of complete hysteria, somehow managed to scream, "Who are you!?"

Jason found that he could move and stepped between the charging man and the others.

Karen and the others began to back toward the kitchen, with the exception of Alex, who remained frozen in fear.

"Alex! Come on!" Theresa cried.

Alex stumbled backward, keeping his gaze constantly fixed on the strange intruder. In her hysteria, Theresa slowly backed into the kitchen.

Jason barked at the others, "Get her out of there!" He then motioned them toward the stairs, unwilling to give in to the mounting fear.

Laura and Karen grabbed Theresa by the arms and dragged her out of the kitchen.

The stranger stepped within striking distance of Alex and stared at him coldly. Alex remained frozen, only able to sheepishly stare back at the threat before him.

The bizarre vision of a man swung his weapon with considerable force, grazing Alex, who finally managed to respond and avoid a deadly blow. "You first!" He took another swing that would have cleanly removed Alex's head if a quick-thinking Jason had not managed to pull him out of the way.

"Somebody help us!" Theresa cried as she fell further back with Laura and Karen beside her.

Karen looked at Laura, somehow intuiting that she alone might have an understanding of what was happening. "What is this?"

Laura had no time to respond.

As the attacker made another move toward Alex, Jason gathered his resolve and rushed him. He slammed into the man at full speed, knocking him several steps backwards. The man fell over, hitting his head on the corner of a solid wood coffee table. He went still, apparently unconscious from the blow.

Laura wasted no time moving to action after she saw their assailant on the ground, "Karen, get your cell phone. If you can get a signal, call 911. I'll watch Theresa."

Jason moved back to his wounded friend, staring at him blankly. "I can't believe it. This is no joke."

Karen moved over to the dining table to grab her cell phone. Something caught her eye, and she looked up to see two hooded individuals looking in from the side windows of the cabin. "Look!"

Everyone else looked up and saw the peculiar sight at the window. A look of recognition crossed Laura's face.

"We have to get out of here! Come on. We're going back down the mountain, now."

Karen and the others abandoned their intentions of running upstairs and quickly headed for the front door instead, followed by

Laura, who stopped briefly to grab the tablet from the dining table. As Laura followed the others out of the door, she took one last look at the windows and realized that the strange visitors were no longer in sight.

Karen paved the way, leading their group toward the van. When she reached it, she was shocked to see that the tires had been slashed to shreds. Reeling from shock and disappointment, she could only turn to Jason and utter, "Oh, no."

The others arrived at her side and immediately realized the same thing Karen had. Their best means of escape was now utterly worthless. They only had one spare tire and little or no time.

"Screw us!" Jason groaned as he punched the side of the van.

Theresa continued to give in to hysteria, looking around furtively for any sign of the people they had seen at the window. "What are we going to do?"

Jason walked past the van, trying to get a good view of the dirt road that led down the mountainside from the cabin. "We have to get down the mountain. On foot if we have to...."

"But not that way," Laura said with a preternatural sense of calm.

Everyone looked up and saw two more mysterious hooded figures in robes standing thirty or forty feet down the road.

Jason responded in kind, "Yeah, I was about to point that out."

Laura took on a more commanding tone, trying to provide some leadership to the little band she had reluctantly joined on this trip to the ridge. "Through the woods then. Let's go. Now."

Laura led them into the woods. As she did so, Karen attempted to use the cell phone, dialing 911. The crestfallen look on her face revealed the failure of her attempt. "Great. No signal. A lot of help this piece of shit is going to be."

"Let's just get out of here," moaned Theresa. "That's all I want to do. Just get out of here."

"We will," Jason said, trying to sound more confident than he felt. "We took care of one of them. We can take care of the rest if we have to."

Laura said nothing but patted Theresa's arm.

* * *

About fifteen minutes later, Laura and the others stopped to catch their breath. They had been moving down the mountain as quickly as they dared for fear of falling and breaking their necks. They had traveled in total silence to that point.

Jason broke the silence as he looked around for any sight of their attackers, "Shit. I just can't believe this."

Theresa was calming slightly, "What do we do now? We haven't seen them since we left the cabin. Maybe they aren't following us."

"I have an idea," Laura said.

"What are you thinking?" Karen piped up, a slight air of mistrust in her voice. Some intuition was beginning to suggest to her that Laura knew more about what was happening than she had said.

"There's a cave not far from here. I think it's our only hope for protection," Laura suggested.

Jason suddenly caught on to Karen's growing skepticism, "How the Hades do you know that? You said you had never been on Miller's Ridge before."

"I think we should worry about that later."

"No. I want to know. We need to know what you're leading us into," Jason rebuffed.

Laura gathered herself and calmly addressed the others, unable to avoid their perplexed faces as she spoke. "Alright. I lied. I have been up here before. Lots of times. I know this place like the back of my hand. I've been coming up here once a year looking for answers to what happened to my mother and other things...."

Karen broke the disturbed silence after Laura's nonchalant confession, "Why did you lie to us? You could have told us this stuff."

Jason growled, "She knew there was danger up here. That's why."

Karen continued, "Laura, are these the same people who killed your mother?"

"I think so."

Theresa turned her back to the others,

staring out into the darkness surrounding them. The light from their cell phones and a flashlight Jason managed to grab faded into near blackness within a few yards under the evening's half moon. "Oh, just freaking great! What are we supposed to do?"

Laura tried to calm her voice, but what she had to say didn't lend itself well to placid conversation, "But people may be the wrong choice of words...."

Jason laughed despite himself, "Don't give me that shit! The guy I knocked out in there was real enough. No more ghost stories. Just tell us how to get down this mountain and back into town."

"Like I said, we have to go toward this cave. It's straight down the mountain from here. When we reach it, we can find protection there if we need it. If not, we can just keep going until we reach town."

Jason began pacing, unable to decide what to do. "I don't know why we should listen to you. You brought us up here, knowing there was danger. Why did you do that?"

Theresa, for some reason, felt the need to

set the facts straight, perhaps as a way to gather herself. "She didn't bring us up here. Alex did."

"Or did he?" piped up Karen. "Somehow, I think your desires got into our heads, Laura. I don't know if you meant to or not, but I do think you're the one who led us up here."

Theresa looked at Laura, thoroughly confused, "Didn't you care that we might be in danger?"

"I have answers to find. I've never come up here alone before, and nobody I brought with me ever got hurt before."

Jason stopped his pacing and made up his mind, "Screw this. Let's just get down this mountain before I have to kill some hooded freaks."

There wasn't much else to be said. With that, they all followed Laura down the mountainside in the direction of the cave, not knowing what might lie in wait for them along the way or whether they could trust the one leading them there.

CHAPTER 10

In Maggie View, Anna and Elise sat on the quaint front porch of their house, sipping cold drinks to combat the summer heat that persisted long after sundown. Anna somehow couldn't relax and enjoy the view as she had on so many nights before.

"I'm a little worried about our young friends, she said."

"Why?" asked Elise, turning to her friend.

"I don't have a good feeling, and you know me and my feelings."

"Yes, they're usually right. People go up on that ridge all the time, though. They typically come back."

"Typically," Anna said, "not always..."

"Do you have any way to contact them?"

"I'm sure they have cell phones, but I didn't get their numbers, did you?" asked Anna.

"No. Those things won't work on the ridge anyway. Let's just keep a close watch on those feelings of yours. If they get worse, we'll send someone up to check on them. There isn't much else we can do."

"If they get much worse, I don't think there's gonna be anyone left to check on."

Anna and Elise smiled and nodded at a young couple strolling by on the sidewalk, but their thoughts were now entirely turned in the direction of their new friends on the mountain. They knew there was danger on the ridge, but they hadn't expected it to be stirred by the presence of Laura and the others. Perhaps there was something they were missing about this group, they both thought, but neither of them said so at that moment. They would find out soon enough.

* * *

In the dense woods of Miller's Ridge, Laura and the others were moving quickly through the trees in the direction Laura had chosen.

Karen had a sudden thought. "Laura, Why did you grab that tablet when we left the cabin?"

"Someone or something has a sick sense of humor. The verses we heard coming from this thing were sent to let us know they're coming for us. When we hear them again, at least this time, we'll be prepared."

"Prepared for what?" Theresa blurted incredulously.

Laura could only respond, "More of the same."

"I can't take this. Please just get me out of here." Theresa was beginning to shake from fear of their potential pursuers.

Jason lost his cool, nearly yelling at Laura, "That's bullshit. Just stop it. All you're doing is scaring Theresa. Nobody is coming after us. We'll be down this mountain in an hour or two, and everyone will be fine."

"I hope you're right."

"Of course I'm right," Jason said, not paying attention to where he was going. At that, Jason lost his footing and began to slide down a steep hillside. Suddenly, he rolled over the edge of a shear drop-off and fell well over twenty feet to the ground below. The others heard him cry out in pain and carefully moved to a point from which they could see him below.

Theresa cried out, "Jason! Are you OK?"

They were all relieved to hear him respond, Yeah, I think so."

Jason attempted to stand up and hobbled on one ankle. "Ow! I think I sprained my ankle.... Or maybe I broke something. And my ribs hurt. I got the wind knocked out of me pretty good."

Laura shouted down, "I'd say you're lucky if that's all that's wrong. Can you climb back up here?"

Jason surveyed the area around him and realized that the hillside remained lofty and steep as far as he could see. It also arced away from the direction in which they had been walking.

"No. No way," he said, "Probably not even if my ankle wasn't hurt."

Theresa felt oddly calmed by the fact that their predicament seemed to be worsening, perhaps because the others were now sharing a bit more of her fear. "Is there any way we can go down?" she asked quietly.

"I don't see how without a rope," replied Karen, looking at Laura and Alex for some manner of additional insight but receiving only frustrated head shakes.

Theresa leaned closer to the edge and nearly fell over herself. Moving quickly, Laura grabbed her, followed by Karen. They pulled her away from the edge, sighing their relief as they managed to do so.

They heard Jason yelling from below. "Be careful up there. Just keep going, and I'll meet you somewhere down the line. Either that or I will see you back in town."

"No. We can't do that," said Theresa, "We can't go without him."

"We have to," Alex responded. "Believe me. I don't want to, but we are going to break our necks if we try to climb down."

Laura yelled down to their friend below, "OK, Jason. Just try to keep your bearings, and we'll meet up in a little while."

"Right. I don't think I can get lost. I will follow the hillside and probably end up leveling out with you guys in a mile or two."

"Be safe, Jason," Theresa yelled down.

Alex followed suit, "Yeah, man. We will meet up soon."

"Don't worry," Jason called up as he began to limp along the hillside from down below. He believed the others wouldn't survive an attack without him, and he moved as quickly as he could, determined to rejoin his friends.

* * *

Several minutes later, Laura led the others into a clearing by a shallow pond of some fifteen feet in diameter. She stopped and sat down, expecting the others to follow suit. They were too nervous to sit. They stood and cautiously caught their breath.

Theresa looked down at Laura, "I'm getting tired. How much further is it to this cave? Please tell me just around the corner."

"About seven or eight miles, then another mile or two from there to town."

Theresa grimaced. If they were still being chased, how could they make it that far, to begin with? They were getting tired, and Laura was the only one who was familiar with the ridge.

And without Jason, what would happen if... what chance would they have?

"What were you talking about when you said this cave would protect us?" asked Karen, "How can it possibly do that if these creeps are after us?"

"It's a sacred place. It should ward off unclean spirits."

Theresa released a nervous giggle, "This is ridiculous. We're being chased by lunatics, not ghosts."

Karen offered the best consolation she could, "Either way, it's a place to hide if we need it."

Laura stood up as Theresa wandered close to the edge of the pond. "I'm so thirsty. Do you think this water is safe to drink?" Theresa asked.

Karen walked over, followed by the others. "At this point, I'm not worried about pond water quality."

"Oh, yeah. I guess we might as well risk it."

They all knelt down to cup water in their hands and take a drink. As Laura did so, she set the tablet on the ground behind them. "Tastes good to me," she said.

Suddenly, the voice of a woman emerged from the tablet. It was a beautiful voice that could have soothed but terrified instead.

The corpse of great Caesar lies bloody there upon the ground,
life spilling from within.

"Shit. Here we go again," said Karen.

Theresa leaned against Alex in fear as the verses continued to pour out of the device on the ground.

Great signs did precede such betrayal,
arriving from a realm unknown.
The darkened streets of Rome displayed sights strange to her people.
Citizens stood wrapped in flames.
Birds of prey and eager lions craved the human carnage destined to appear.
The mouths of graves opened to speak of impending change,
loosing all their shades,

*and the night sky was so full of odd lights
that prophecies of doom could be read beneath them.*

The voice suddenly ceased. A tense moment passed as the three of them sat dumbfounded.

Alex spoke up, "Does anyone see anything?"

The others shook their heads.

Karen tried to process what was happening in a rational fashion, pushing aside the fear and focusing on the meaning of the words. "OK. So, does anyone know what that was supposed to mean?"

"I can't tell you. It wasn't anything that I ever wrote. I know that much. At the moment, all I can think of is there is danger, and it has something to do with the past," Laura said, calmly.

Theresa moved close to Alex and grabbed him by the arm, "Nothing's happening. Maybe it's over. Maybe they'll leave us alone now."

"No. I don't think so," Laura said. "I think something is happening, just maybe not right here."

"Jason?" asked Alex.

Laura sighed, "Yeah. There's no reason to think that the messages of doom couldn't apply to him instead of us for the moment."

Alex kicked at the ground. "Shit. If he is in danger, we'd never find him in time to help."

"Whatever is happening, we have to keep moving," Karen said, and they all followed Laura out of the clearing.

* * *

Not far away, Jason began to fight his way up an incline that would likely lead to finding his friends if he could endure the pain in his ankle and side that had him wincing with every step. Twisting the ankle again, he grimaced and cursed, "Fuck! Screw me and this mountain."

He managed to keep from falling over and then carefully sat down to rub his wounded ankle and catch his breath. As he sat, he looked up and noticed a vision of beauty moving toward him through the trees, a slender young woman with dark skin and pronounced cheekbones. She wore the traditional garb of the Cherokee people and seemed to float toward him with an unnatural grace. She wore a necklace and hat reminiscent of 1920s mainstream American fashion that clashed with the rest of her attire, but in Jason's view of her, all was in perfect symmetry. He was entranced by her presence, lost in a spell that she seemed to cast over him.

Jason stood, no longer noticing the pain. "Hello," he managed to muster.

"Hello," the lovely girl responded. Then, she moved close to him – close enough to take him into her arms.

He did not resist, could not resist. He could only manage to say, "Can you help me? I took a fall, and I'm seriously hurt."

"Come to me. I can help you."

He surrendered to her embrace, and she kissed him. He could think of nothing else but her arms, her lips, and the lust that grew within him.

The young woman moved deftly to produce a dagger from behind her back. She thrust it into Jason's heart. He dropped to the ground, desire still clearly visible in his eyes.

She sat beside him and cradled him as he died. She smiled at him warmly, "You see. I've helped you. I've ended your pain."

Then she leaned over and kissed him again.

CHAPTER 11

Anna and Elise sat in the kitchen, eating sandwiches and continuing to sip glasses of tea. Elise broke a pervasive silence that had been with them since they stepped back inside the house.

"What's wrong?"

Anna spoke through a mouth full of bacon, lettuce, and tomato. "My feelings about this aren't getting any better. Something's wrong up there."

"What should we do?"

"Call Sheriff Johnson and tell him he needs to send somebody up there to check on those kids."

"Because you have a feeling?"

"No," Anna protested. "We'll tell him we got a frantic cell phone call from them, and their phone cut off before they could explain what was wrong."

"And what if nothing is wrong, Anna?"

"We'll just say we must have misunderstood them. What's he gonna do, arrest us? Our tour may be the best business in this town. Besides, I've known him forever."

"I don't know, Anna."

"Do you want to go up there?"

"Hell no."

"Then get me the phone."

Elise groaned, put her sandwich down and walked over to grab a cell phone from the kitchen counter. "Life sometimes gets interesting in the summer, doesn't it?"

* * *

Alex and the others followed Laura, rapidly moving in the direction of a hope in which they didn't entirely believe. They grew tired from the pace they were keeping, and their thoughts drifted to their friend and what might have become of him.

Suddenly, they found themselves in

another small clearing and saw that there was an old, apparently abandoned shack there. It was in a terrible state of disrepair. Somehow, a big hole had been torn into its side.

Karen stepped close to it, "What kind of shack is that?"

"I don't know. It's weird. I never came across this place before," Laura answered, peering inside the shack through the broken-down wall.

Karen followed suit, "You don't think anyone could still be living there, do you?"

Laura seemed suddenly lost in thought and absentmindedly replied, "I doubt it." She was beginning to feel a familiar presence, something from her past that always seemed to be tied to the mystery of her origins.

Together, they all walked inside to have a look around, each of them hoping to find some implement of survival inside or that the tiny dwelling might at least offer a place to hide. They quickly scoured the dilapidated shack and discovered nothing but an old, rotten table and some broken dishes on the floor.

Laura wandered off to the far corner by

herself and bent over to pick something up.

"What have you got?" asked Karen.

"It's an old fishing knife. This might be worth having. We'll see." Laura handed the knife to Karen. "You hang on to it. I'm already keeping up with the tablet."

Suddenly, they heard a rustling sound outside of the shack. They exchanged frightened looks and slowly moved toward the hole in the side wall.

Before they could exit, an older man stepped through the front door. He appeared to them all to be a shabbily dressed hermit who must have actually been living there. He recoiled in surprise but gathered himself and spoke to them calmly.

"Oh, visitors. I haven't had any of those in a while."

Laura cautiously moved forward and responded, "Who are you?"

"I live here. Don't worry. You don't have anything to be afraid of. Do I?"

Karen chuckled despite herself, "No."

Theresa and Alex responded in harmony, "What do you mean, no?"

"You folks sound like you've seen some kind of trouble."

Laura and the others recounted everything they had experienced to the shabby-looking man, and he listened intently. After they were done, he gave them all an unreadable look but responded, "I don't know what to make of what you're telling me, but I'll be glad to lead you folks the rest of the way down. I try to get to town about once a month anyway. I'm sure we'll be fine."

Theresa breathed a sigh of enormous relief. "Thank you. Thank you so much. I just want to get back to campus and forget I ever came to this mountain."

They all nearly jumped out of their skin as the tablet fired to life again, and the same woman's voice began to recite odd verses over the speakers. Theresa's brief moment of relief rapidly withdrew and turned into a familiar, cold terror.

Into the woods with you,
discovering the tender arms of the night,
Exquisite shade and shadow

"Believe us now?" Karen asked the hermit as
the voice continued.
We saw only hints of that vast soup,
the distant lights above.
I thought I would never leave the folds of such
beauty.
I guess I'm still recalling the night
we slipped out of our rags and into our skin.
The touch of you, the taste of you,
your scent became a verse of ecstasy,
the night a mystery in your arms.

There was total silence for a moment as
the voice ceased.

"What does it mean?" Karen asked, her
voice sounding as timid as the gentle rustling of
leaves in the surrounding trees.

Laura answered, "The arrival of lovers."
The tone of her voice indicated something far
more sinister than her words.

The hermit looked at them all as if they
were crazy. "Come on. It's just words from a toy
machine."

"No. It's more than that," Laura insisted.
She looked up and was the first to see the young

couple, Darren and Cindy, bursting through the trees. Behind them appeared two members of the Compendium wearing robes, a man and a woman. Their hoods were pulled back, their faces burned and scarred.

The disfigured man and woman chased Darren and Cindy toward the shack. They carried large swords with serrated edges on one side of the blades.

Theresa screamed and beckoned the others to follow her into the woods. She paused at the edge of the tree line and nervously waited for them.

Cindy cried out as she and Darren were overtaken by the compendium members, "Help us!" But it was too late.

In a flash of steel beneath the moonlight, Cindy and Darren were cut down by the wicked swords the man and woman wielded with seemingly inhuman strength. As they fell to the ground, they were cut to pieces before Alex or any of the others could even reach them.

"This prey is sweet!" hissed the ragged voice of the woman.

"They belong," said the man, kneeling to

finish off Darren with a downward thrust of his sword.

"What the hell is this?" shouted the hermit. "What have you people brought to this place?"

"We didn't bring anything that wasn't already here," Laura bemoaned as they ran out of the clearing.

The cloaked woman looked up and watched them run away, savoring her kills and thought of the carnage to follow. They would have the others soon enough.

* * *

Laura and the others, including the hermit, ran out of the trees a few minutes later into an open area. Laura was the first to see the cave at the other end of the field.

"Look, there it is!"

Weary and uncertain, they all ran toward the greatest security they had seen since fleeing the cabin.

Suddenly, not far behind them, the robed man and woman burst out of the trees and began chasing them.

The robed man quickly approached,

and Laura turned to face him. As she stood her ground, the man abruptly fell to his knees and grabbed his head in his hands.

"Arrrgh! It hurts!" the man cried.

Laura continued to run. They reached the cave's mouth and ran inside the shallow hold.

Only several feet stood between them and their pursuers.

The hermit pulled out a lighter and looked around at the cave walls. The rugged walls were covered in old drawings of symbols and images that seemed to be of Native American origin.

"I've been here before. This was a sacred place to the Cherokee," he said. "I don't understand why, but they marked it for some reason."

Theresa and Karen hid behind the hermit as the robed man and woman approached the entrance and stopped. The curious and deadly pair surveyed the people inside with cold and merciless looks on their faces, but they did not enter.

The woman laughed softly in her hoarse tone. "You will not be protected for long. You are but meat for a feast."

The two of them turned away and walked back toward the woods, disappearing into the trees in disturbing silence.

Laura and the others breathed deeply. All but Laura were shocked that the Compendium members had been unwilling or unable to pursue them into the little cave.

Both the hermit and Karen examined the symbols on the cave walls. Theresa sat against the wall, and Laura stared out into the field.

"I'd like to know what the hell those things were," the hermit barked.

"You live here. Haven't you ever seen them before?" Karen nervously asked of the strange companion they had picked up by the rotting shack.

"If I had, do you think I would still be living here? I never saw this shit till you people came along. Just what have you gotten me into?"

Theresa moaned, "We're all about to die. That's what we've gotten you into."

Karen moved over to comfort Theresa, and Alex joined her. They huddled up, sharing warmth and strength.

"Don't give up," Karen admonished her

friends. "We're only a couple of miles from town now. We can make it. Right, Laura?"

"Maybe."

"Laura, why wouldn't they come in here?" Karen asked, now uncertain of everything she had embraced as reality just a few hours before.

"Like he said, this is a sacred place."

"What happened to that one in the field?" asked the hermit, staring Laura down. "He was screaming bloody murder back there."

Theresa nodded in Laura's direction. "She did it. I don't know how, but she did it. She's tied to this place and those monsters, and she didn't tell us before we came up here."

Laura looked at them but said nothing. Inside, her emotions were churning. Had she brought them all to their deaths? Had she been brought here by some force she still didn't understand? If so, her companions were merely unfortunate bystanders despite the fact that they had seemed to be the vehicle of her own arrival on Miller's Ridge.

Karen interrupted Laura's thoughts, "How did you do that?"

Laura stared out into the darkness, "I've always had a sense of what lies underneath the surface, how to manipulate and explore things with my mind. It's grown more powerful the older I've gotten. I've never done anything like that before, but somehow I knew I could cause him pain."

Karen could only respond, "I don't understand this."

"I do. She drew us here. To die," said Theresa, her mind and heart churning with fear.

Alex finally spoke, "Look. We brought her here. We have to stop blaming each other and work to get down this mountain alive. We're not far from town now. We can make it."

"Listen to the young man," directed the hermit. "Sacred or not, we need to get out of this cave and make it to town before more of them show up."

* * *

As Laura and the others stood in the sacred cave, longing to be off of the mountain, two police officers made their way up to the cabin in search of them. Bobby and Roy were the two youngest officers in the small Maggie View police force, both of them skinny as rails and sporting buzz cuts that did nothing to make them appear more intimidating as they had intended.

As they entered the cabin, they immediately spotted the strange man still lying unconscious on the floor. Beside the man rested the axe with just a trace of blood on it from the earlier attack on Alex.

As they drew closer, Bobby turned to Roy, "Oh, shit. I've never seen anything like this. Who the hell is this guy?"

Roy drew his gun and responded, "I don't know, but I think he's still alive. Guess the ghost tour ladies were right. Something bad has gone down here."

Bobby cautiously reached down and turned the man over to get a better look at his face.

Roy was shocked at what he saw, "I can't believe it. Do you know who this is?"

"Yeah, it's Paul Canter. He disappeared up here over two years ago."

"That's exactly right," said Roy, bewildered by their discovery.

Suddenly, the man's eyes opened, and

his arms jerked around briefly before he went still again.

Bobby jumped backward and instinctively drew his gun from its holster as well. "Shit. What am I doing? We're not going to have any trouble from Paul." Bobby reached down to check the man's pulse. He felt nothing but a faint trace of a heartbeat. "I don't know. He must be in some kind of coma. This is loony."

"What about the rest of those kids?" Roy asked.

"They must be on the way down the mountain."

"But we didn't see them on the road."

"I know," Bobby said with concern apparent in his voice, "Something must have driven them into the woods. Get on the radio and let them know to start a search from the bottom up."

* * *

Laura and the others stood nervously by the entrance to the small cave. They were considering making a break for their lives down the mountain toward town.

"Look, I didn't bring anybody up here to

get killed," Laura said, breaking a tense silence among the group.

"Forget all that," Karen said, "The point is, how are we going to get down the rest of the way without getting cut to ribbons?"

The hermit studied Laura in a way that was beginning to make her uncomfortable, "Can you use that shit to stop those two if they come after us again?"

"I don't know."

Theresa implored, "I'm not leaving this cave. They couldn't come in here. Why should we leave?"

"I didn't like what she said about us not being protected for long. I get the feeling they'll be back soon, and this cave won't be enough to stop them," Laura said, peering in the direction of the trees for any sign of compendium members.

Karen agreed, "Me too. We're so close to town now. There has to be a way to make it."

"And there's a house not more than half a mile down the mountain from here," the hermit said, finally looking away from Laura.

Alex blurted, "What? Why didn't you

say that before?"

"I didn't think about it. They're bound to have a phone too. And probably weapons to boot."

"That does it," Karen commanded, "We're going."

Theresa sat down against the cave wall. "You guys go and call for help. I'm not going out there again."

Laura spoke up, "I don't know if it's such a good idea for you to stay here by yourself, Theresa."

"I'll be alright here. They won't come into the cave. Just go. Hurry!"

With that, they all looked at each other and silently determined to make their run for survival. Laura sat the tablet down beside Theresa, and they all bolted out of the cave.

"Hurry!" Theresa cried out, too terrified to go but almost equally terrified to stay behind. What had happened to them this night? How much simpler and safer their world had seemed just hours before.

Laura and the others made it back into the trees without glimpsing any of their mysterious pursuers. They ran at breakneck speed, sighting the house, with its windows lit, in what seemed like a moment later. As they slowed down, they heard a sudden shriek behind them. Fearing the worst, they turned to discover Karen had merely twisted her ankle.

Laura helped Karen up, "Are you OK.?"

Karen winced a bit as she stood but showed no signs of stopping, "I'll be a lot better as soon as we get inside that house and lock the doors."

Laura shuddered as they arrived, knowing somehow that Theresa, alone in the cave, faced impending danger. At that moment, it seemed inconceivable to her that they had allowed Theresa to stay behind, but she couldn't dwell on it now.

Theresa's friends wouldn't be seeing her again. Laura felt certain of that.

CHAPTER 12

Theresa sat with her back against the wall in the cave, staring straight across at the opposite wall, not looking out into the moonlit field beyond the cave's mouth. She quietly whispered to herself, drawing an odd comfort from the sound of her own gentle words, "It's OK. They'll find the house and be back here soon. Just wait. Just think about being back in town."

The unknown woman's voice suddenly piped through the tablet's speakers again. Theresa's calm was shattered. She knew the warning was for her, echoing through the darkness, echoing through some forbidden space between the world she knew and a world she desperately longed to escape...

Onto a murky, ethereal back,
my wayward psyche climbs,
"Stop!" Theresa cried, but the voice would not.
Making tangent contact
with the soon outstretched wings
of this dim carrier,
this breathing ferry on a course to despair.
Oh, on a day such as this one,
how the raven's coal darkness strives to torment me,
its conniving song, a blunt melody
drawn from times certain march forward.

As the warning ceased, Theresa moved to the front of the cave and looked out into the field beyond, frantically jerking her head from side to side in an effort to see if any attackers were approaching. She saw nothing but the dripping of moonlight between the trees like melancholy streams of tears falling from some celestial beings who could do nothing to help her here.

Suddenly, Theresa heard a voice in the cave behind her. She turned around in cold terror to see the young woman who killed Jason earlier. The woman was accompanied by three other hooded individuals. These three showed signs of the facial mutations and scars they had seen on other members of the compendium.

"If you're wondering what this one means," said the young woman, whose voice Theresa now recognized as the one emanating from the tablet, "it means you were never really safe in this cave. Don't worry, dear. It will be over soon."

Theresa crawled backward, crying in fear. She began to get up and run away, but she was set upon by all four of the mysterious beings before she could escape. They tore into her with daggers, swinging with great ferocity until they were all soaked in her blood.

"Now we have a lot more company, don't we?" asked the young woman, stepping away from Theresa as the others continued to stab and slice at her. "Just like the master wanted."

* * *

As Theresa slipped out of the mortal world, a bunch of police officers and other local residents gathered at the bottom of the mountain with flashlights and other equipment.

The sheriff of Maggie View signaled them to begin moving upward.

The sheriff was a taciturn man, barrel-chested and bald. He made his directions brief, "You all know what to do. Keep your eyes open and contact me if you find anything!"

Everyone began moving into the woods and up the hillside, eager to play their part in rescuing a group of lost college kids facing some unidentified danger. A deputy named Carl approached the sheriff, panting already from his trips between official vehicles to gather equipment. He had been so busy trying to corral volunteers that he didn't even know what they were volunteering to do.

"What exactly are we looking for, sheriff?"

"Three or four college kids, hopefully alive."

The deputy was taken aback, being unaccustomed to anything particularly dramatic occurring in town. "Why wouldn't they be alive?"

The sheriff grimaced despite himself, "Because there's been some trouble up on

Miller's Ridge. Wouldn't be the first time someone had gone missing or ran into some danger up there..."

"Damn. I didn't know."

"Stick around here very long, and you will know."

* * *

Laura knocked on the front door of the house, which was a rustic, one-story cabin house with a storage building sitting off to one side. The hermit stood behind her, along with Alex and Karen.

They immediately heard someone approaching the door from within. A woman's voice spoke up from the other side.

"Can I help you?"

"Yes, ma'am, Laura said, "We have a hurt girl here, and we need to use a phone to call the police."

"Who are you?"

Laura answered politely, "We were in town on vacation. Do you know Anna and Elise? We stayed with them last night."

The door creaked loudly as it slowly opened.

A late middle-aged woman looked out and surveyed them. She wore a house dress and a pair of thick glasses. "My name is Dorris Venters. Come on in. Let's take a look at this hurt girl."

As they walked through the door, and Dorris attempted to assess what someone like the hermit would be doing with a group of young people. Laura and her friends were just happy to see the front door close behind them, and they quickly embraced this modest piece of civilization.

Alex sat on a couch with his face buried in his hands, certain that he wouldn't see his roommate again. Jason was his best friend and often felt like the big brother he never had. Something beyond Alex's understanding had happened to Jason this night, and he was trying to make sense of it. A kind of shock was settling into his psyche.

Karen and Laura explained the evening's bizarre incidents to Dorris while she was putting a wrap on Karen's ankle. Easy listening music played on a small radio sitting on a coffee table in the living room. The hermit just sat down on the table beside it and stared as if lost in some distant but somewhat happier time.

Dorris said little as the girls explained and then looked up at Karen with warm empathy. "Better?"

"Yes. Thank you so much."

"You're welcome. Now, I don't have a phone, but I do have a two-way radio out in my storage shed. I also keep my emergency services scanner out there. I listen to it more than the radio. It's more interesting."

"Could you use that to call the police?" Laura asked.

"Sure, honey. I can get through to them on that. They aren't much of a police force, but they do tend to come when called upon. I'll go do it right now."

"Thank you again."

Dorris walked out of the house, and Karen gave Laura a concerned look.

Laura answered the unasked question. "She's been safe here this long. I think she knows what she's doing."

The hermit jumped into the discussion, "We're not that far from town here. If she gets hold of the police, they will be up here in a few minutes."

* * *

Dorris made her way to the shed, slightly apprehensive about the short journey but confident enough that she would be safe on the grounds of her own home. After all, she had never known any trouble here.

She quickly raised the dispatcher Mary and was surprised to find that the police were already aware there was trouble on the mountain. "You mean the police are already on the way up here?"

"They sure are, and a bunch of volunteers, too," Mary informed. "I'd send somebody straight to your house, but there's no one left to send."

"That's OK. I think we'll be alright till they all make their way up here. Goodnight."

"Goodnight, Dorris."

With that, Dorris sat down the microphone and stood up with the intention of returning to her guests with comforting news. Suddenly, the door burst open. The robed man and woman who had chased Laura and the others earlier stepped inside and stared at Dorris like cornered prey.

"Who are you?" Dorris managed.

Making no response, they pinned her to the floor and tore her to shreds with daggers. As Dorris lay dying, a coppery taste filled her mouth, the pain at some point ceased, and she began to understand. A harvest was taking place on Miller's Ridge, a transition of souls to somewhere else, a place that could be reached from the mountain but only on the rarest of occasions. It, or the beings who controlled it, had never before allowed the entrance of so many at once.

It was that girl, the girl now standing in her house. She was like fuel for the gateway between one place and another. She had not intended to cause such misery, only to solve the riddles of her origins. If only she understood her own origins, perhaps she could stop it. Perhaps she could reverse what was happening. There was such power in that girl, Dorris thought, as she breathed her last breath and straddled a mystical line between two worlds.

Then she understood entirely.

* * *

Back in Dorris's house, the others were all standing or pacing, feeling on edge as they waited for Dorris to return.

Karen found herself driven to distraction by the strains of mellow seventies tunes emerging from the radio but couldn't bring herself to focus on changing the station or just shutting the radio off. "This music is driving me nuts," she blurted, but she knew she would take any music over silence under the circumstances.

"Do you think they're done with us, whoever they are?" the mountain hermit asked, surveying Laura closely.

"No, I don't."

"Yeah. I didn't think so," he responded.

"What can we do?" Karen asked, pacing to work the soreness out of her ankle and the tension out of her nerves.

"Live long enough for the police to show up if we're lucky," Laura said, "I hate to say this, but I have a strong sense that Theresa's dead already."

Alex piped up, "Come on, you don't...."

Suddenly, the music on the radio was

interrupted by a man's voice. It resonated through the room in a fashion that seemed impossible, given the diminutive nature of the radio itself. The hermit stared at the radio in disbelief.

I am a night watchman, forsaking daylight's pleasantries.
Jet-marbled hours of evening
escort my soul-prophetic
to the habitation of perturbed spirits.
Choleric eaglets, they hang against an ashen sky,
forming a regal phalanx on a supple sea extraordinary.
And I, adrift in that ethereal fluid,
suspended in a deluge of clarity,
overhear sacred proclamations of hope
that pledge redemption from shadowy cries of unrest.

Karen bemoaned, "We get rid of the tablet, and still, they follow us. Who are these people, Laura? What are they?

"This voice has come to me in dreams. I can see the face that goes with it. It's like the power behind all of this has just revealed itself to us."

"Why, so we can know who's about to kill us?" Karen asked without really expecting an answer.

"Kill nothing. I'm not dying like this," Alex said while walking to one of the windows. "We have to pull it together and just get to town or ride it out until the police get here. I don't understand what's happening, but that's all we have to do."

Laura joined Alex by the window and saw what neither of them wanted to see. Several of the members of the compendium were approaching the house. The young woman who killed Jason was there, the robed man and woman, and various others in similar attire. They all held weapons, mostly wicked-looking knives. Laura ran to the other side of the room and looked out. "We've got problems in all directions."

"They're here again?" Karen asked nervously.

"And more than two this time."

The hermit calmly sized Laura up, "Try

to stop them."

"I don't even know how I did that before," Laura said. "It just happened." Lurking beyond her own fear was her fear for the others and her guilt that she had somehow drawn them all here.

"Well, if you can't do it again, we're gonna have to fight 'em the hard way. Otherwise, we're dead."

The attack came on the side of the house that faced up the mountain first. One of the compendium members was ramming into the door in an attempt to break it down.

An arm burst through the window on the other side of the house. Wasting no time in responding, Karen grabbed a fishing knife, ran to the window, and sliced the arm. The arm recoiled, but no cry of pain was heard.

Once again, an arm burst in. This time, Karen stabbed the awkward fishing knife straight through the attacker's forearm, temporarily pinning him to the wall.

"Good," cried Laura, "Find something else to fight with." She was hoping that whatever power had sprung forth from somewhere within stayed in check this time. She wanted to defend herself and the others, but she was more terrified of whatever had happened before than she was of their strange attackers.

Karen and the hermit began frantically searching around the room for anything else they could use in their defense. As Laura watched, the attacker in the window managed to free himself. He peered in and stared at her with both hatred and reverence.

"No escape," Laura thought she heard him say. But then, she wasn't sure if he had said the words or if she had heard them in her mind.

Laura lunged forward and kicked the man in the face, breaking more glass as she did so and knocking him backwards to the ground. Feeling a shooting pain, she looked down and realized she had a small shard of glass embedded in the side of her foot.

Nearby, Karen discovered a revolver in a coffee table drawer. Seeing it was loaded, she quickly moved toward the window with the gun raised in her somewhat shaky hand. "How bout this?"

Alex barricaded the front door and

looked back to see Karen's newfound weapon. "Now that's what I'm talking about!"

Laura lifted her foot in front of Karen, who grimaced upon seeing the piece of glass and a trickle of blood.

"Pull it out."

Karen obliged Laura, then fired a few rounds from the pistol in the direction of the beings on the other side of the window.

"Did you get any of them?" Laura asked tensely.

"Look."

They both looked out and saw that one of the odd group was lying on the ground with three bullet holes in him. He did not move or make a sound. The pounding on the door suddenly stopped, and there were no other attackers to be seen.

"I think we drove them off," the hermit said.

Laura countered, "No. We haven't seen the last of them. They will never leave till they have what they want."

As if in response, a man's voice boomed out of the radio again.

Movement, disorder, worlds unknown,
hesitation on the wind, destruction in necessity.
Milk of flesh, paranoid in the darkness,
peculiar invasion.
New in regeneration, being awakened,
beauty in the imperfect cities underneath.

"It's a welcome," said Laura.

"To who?" Karen responded, incredulous.

"To me, I think...and to chaos."

Suddenly, the house was assaulted from all sides. Windows shattered all around them, and two doors gave way under the force of the bodies beyond. Karen ran to the coffee table and acquired a few more bullets. She nervously reloaded the revolver. Laura grabbed the fishing knife and stood with the hermit on the other side of the room.

Alex grabbed a walking stick and stood in the middle of the room, bracing for what was to come.

The door by Laura and the hermit gave way, and they were rushed by the robed man and woman, as well as several others.

Karen faced the door on the other side of the house with the gun raised. She fired a couple of rounds through the door, then rushed to open the door and exit the house. She had made her decision. Time to run for the town and not look back.

Karen hit the ground running and ignored the pain in her ankle. She fired wildly, emptying the gun but not hitting any further attackers. Laura and the hermit ran out the door after Karen, but several of the compendium members cut them off so they could not pursue her.

Alex joined them, screaming, "Back to the cave. Come on!"

As they ran, several attackers reached for them and nearly managed to stop them.

There was no way for them to run down the mountain. They could only run back in the direction from which they had come.

Laura yelled at Alex and the hermit as they ran away, "This won't work!"

"There's nowhere else to go!" Alex took the lead but didn't make it far. He was tackled from the side by a large, robed man. Before

Laura could even stop to think how to help him, Alex was lost, fallen victim to the thrust of a wicked dagger deftly wielded by the man.

Laura was nauseous from what she had witnessed, but she ran on, driven by some survival instinct she didn't know she possessed until that moment.

Several minutes later, sucking in pain with every labored breath, Laura and the hermit burst out of the trees, hotly pursued by several of their attackers. The compendium members didn't seem to tire. They seemed to be playing a game with Laura and her unexpected companion. Laura felt they had been allowed to make it to this point.

They had arrived at the clearing by the sacred cave.

Laura stopped, hoping to repeat what she did to the robed man the last time, but nothing happened. Unable to draw forth whatever power lay somewhere within her, she ran for the cave, crying. She was more genuinely frightened than she had ever been in her life, yet she was so frustrated that she just wanted to fight.

They reached the cave no more than twenty feet ahead of their closest pursuers and entered, turning around to face the inevitable.

Laura whispered as she tried to slow her frantic breathing, "Please be safe here." At that moment, she looked down and saw Theresa's mangled body lying against one wall, the tablet lying on her in pieces.

"No, not safe."

The hermit spoke up, "You will always be safe here."

Laura looked at him in confusion, but she was distracted by the imminent arrival of the murderous beings beyond the cave entrance. What the hell was he talking about? At any rate, they were about to find out as the first of the robed freaks arrived at the cave.

* * *

Close to the bottom of the mountain, Karen ran at breakneck speed, her head down, barely able to see anything but what was directly in front of her feet. I can make it. I'm so close, she thought.

She stumbled, her wounded ankle giving way under her. Suddenly, she was clasped in someone's arms. She screamed.

"It's OK, honey. You're alright. I'm the sheriff of Maggie View."

"Oh, thank God," Karen exhaled, looking up to realize she was not captured by one of her pursuers. Karen wrapped her arms around the sheriff and cried.

"Thank you!"

"Where are the others?"

"The cave. You have to get to the cave."

The sheriff turned to a deputy, who stood directly behind him. "Do you know where that is?"

"Sure do," the deputy chirped.

Other men began to appear in the woods around them, volunteers from the town.

"Round up some of these men and get up there. Find out what's going on," the sheriff ordered.

"Yes, sir." With that, the deputy was off to gather some assistance and make his way up the mountainside.

The sheriff took Karen by the arm and led her toward a lady among the volunteers who would walk with her back to town. "Don't worry, honey. Help is here now, and we're gonna do everything we can to get to your friends in a hurry."

It won't be enough, thought Karen. *I can't believe I'm even standing here myself. I left them, and I'm going to have to cope with it for the rest of my life... I'm not even out of college yet, and I'm going to have to live with being the one who lived...*

CHAPTER 13

Looking out from the cave, Laura cast a brief, frightened glance at the people standing just feet away. They peered into the cave, faces lit with evil grins, half phantasms painted against the moonlit night.

Her head suddenly swirled with a vision, an image of a creature in humanoid form emerging through some dark window between another world and her own. It was as if it flew in on invisible wings and landed somewhere nearby.

Laura regained her senses and was shocked to see that the hermit's appearance had totally changed. He was the man she had seen in her dreams when they slept on the nature trail. Jarret. She somehow knew his name. "You! What is this?"

"What you came here for, girl. That's what it is."

Jarret motioned to those outside of the cave, and they backed off, slowly beginning to form a semicircle together near the entrance.

Laura nervously looked out at the attackers and then back at Jarret, "Who are you?"

Jarret evinced a slight grin, "The choreographer of this great performance. It was all for you, Laura."

"All for me? The murder of my friends?"

"You must forgive the crude nature of some of our lesser companions, girl. It was a brutal night. But we prefer to think of it as initiation, not murder."

"An Initiation? To what?"

"To the final expression of what has been awaiting you your entire life."

Laura grew angry, feeling the mysterious energy bubbling to life within her again, "Who decides what has been awaiting me? You?"

"No. You and your fate, Laura. They

decide. You will unite with us before this night is over."

"I don't know about fate, but if I decide, I have nothing to do with this. I don't belong here with these monsters."

Jarret walked silently out of the cave to join the other compendium members. "Laura, the members of the Compendium are but people, not monsters. Spirits joined together here with the power to move between this world and what lies beyond. And you have belonged among us your entire life. Even your mother understood that."

Laura was taken aback. She didn't think any further surprises were possible. "My mother? You knew her?"

"Yes. In my own earthly life, I told her about your powers. She knew what would happen to you. She was well aware that we would seek to join your powers with our own. It was her very spirit that tried to warn you to leave this place as you sat in your newfound friend's parlor in the valley below."

"Then I never had a choice in all of this!"

"Yes, girl. You did. You brought innocent

people here, knowing full well there was danger. Your powers told you of that danger. That callousness has sealed your fate. Tonight you join us."

"But you warned me in my dream. Why would you do that if you've always been a part of this nightmare?"

"More of the performance. It's been a good one, wouldn't you say?"

"Why don't you just move on like all spirits must?"

"We have moved on, just not to what you might expect, not to perdition or to the light. We've moved to a place in between or beyond or right next door...to a place that sometimes even grants us entry to the world in which we once lived....0on rare nights like this one. We bear the scars of our departure from our human lives, but we have found another world worth the painful process of escaping."

Laura stepped out of the cave, knowing that it wouldn't protect her at any rate. "I will not join you! I will not die here tonight!"

"Yes, you will, and no one who joins us ever leaves."

* * *

Outside the cabin, Bobby and Roy stood beside their patrol car, talking with the dispatcher in town.

Roy was relieved by what he was hearing, "So they found one of them?"

"Sure did," he said. "They're looking for the others now."

"Good. When you see the sheriff, tell him we're gonna need some help up here."

"Will do, Roy. Watch out and be careful, boys."

Bobby leaned sideways against the car, "Well, what now?"

"I guess we get an ambulance up here, so they can get Paul back to town, and we can start trying to figure out exactly where he's been for two years."

Suddenly, Paul was on top of them, appearing from nowhere. He swung his terrible axe at Bobby splitting his skull open with a fatal blow.

Roy fell backwards to the ground and struggled to get his pistol out of the holster. As he did so, Paul swung the ax down with great force and buried it in Roy's chest. Paul pulled the ax out as poor Roy squirmed on the ground beneath him. Paul calmly stared off into the woods, sensing what was happening somewhere between the cabin and the bottom of the mountain.

He sensed it as Jason rose from the ground at another part of the mountain, looked around, and began walking slowly away, showing no more signs of pain or injury, only strange markings on his face. He knew Jason wasn't the only one rising to a new reality.

* * *

Theresa got up and walked out of the cave, still bloodied but showing no signs of pain.

Laura looked at her friend, and a tear streamed down her cheek as she began to process the sadness of a lost life. "I'm sorry."

Theresa gave her a perplexed look. "Don't be sorry. We are together always. You haven't lost me, Laura."

"No, you're wrong. Only until the final judgment. There will be a price to pay for what's been done here, for the door that's been opened."

"Don't speak of a price, Laura," Jarret intoned. "None of us knows of any certainty of price or penalty. You belong with us now. You always have."

"No!" Laura screamed.

Laura looked at the robed man and woman, staring intently in an effort to do them harm. They both began screaming and ran away in terror.

"You see, I, too, can call up fear. Or chaos." She raised her hand and stared at another group of would-be attackers. They fell to the ground and began crawling aimlessly, unable to see. "Or recreate the past."

The young woman who had killed Jason suddenly grabbed her chest and fell over in pain.

"Why did you hurt me? This pain was from my former life."

Laura ignored the girl's pleas and stared at Jarret, "I can hurt you, too."

Jarret responded calmly but with a cold tone in his voice, "I know. But I wouldn't have called you here if your powers were greater than our own. The compendium is always stronger than the one, even this one." Jarret looked around him. Suddenly, the others became quiet and began to regroup. They closed in on her.

"Your power will be relished, Laura."

Theresa was the first to move forward and grab Laura, who fought to get free from her.

It was hopeless. As the others forced Laura to the ground, the last thing Laura saw in her natural life was their hands and weapons in the air, ready to strike her.

"Welcome," she heard Jarret say, and then in a flash of strange light that opened the space around her like unseen hands opening an impossible gateway, she saw her mother standing expressionless in a place altogether new to her.

CHAPTER 14

On the following morning, Karen sat in a daze, sipping coffee while Anna and Elise slowly nibbled on breakfast across from her at their small dining table.

"Poor thing. I'm so sorry for what you've been through," Anna comforted.

"It's not your fault," Karen said, "We should have listened and never gone up there. But then, I guess we had to, somehow...."

"You know nobody is ever really going to believe what happened up there but us."

"I know."

"You might as well start making up a story to tell the sheriff," advised Elise with a slight grin.

"Don't worry. I've already started."

Karen rose and walked to the door of the kitchen, wondering to herself if the veil into some other world would ever be lifted for her again.

"You OK?" Anna asked delicately.

"I'm alive if that counts."

"It counts for a lot. I know it seems impossible now, but you'll get over this in time," Elise offered with conviction.

"I doubt it, but I'll take my chances compared with dying in those woods. All I can say is you're in the right business and the right town for it. Laura was drawn up on that ridge for a reason, and us, along with her. Now she's going to be there for a long time." Even as she said it, Karen knew that the mountain wasn't exactly where Laura was, or any of the rest of them, but maybe they would be there from time to time, peering back into the world that had once been their own.

* * *

Years later, Elise drove Anna up the mountainside toward Miller's Ridge. It was a beautiful Spring evening with flowers in bloom, the explosion of warm colors forming a soft and cozy palette against which one could live a quiet life. They passed the country store and kept going upward in the direction of the known as well as the unknown.

Elise glanced over at her friend of so many years, "Are you sure this is the way you want things?"

"Yes. Take me to the ridge. I'm not waiting around for death to walk through my front door – our front door."

"I understand, but you don't know what you're really getting yourself into."

"No, but I feel it. I've felt it ever since that girl came to town all those years ago."

"I don't want to say goodbye to my best friend."

Anna looked at her warmly and smiled, "Neither do I. Maybe we will see each other again."

* * *

Anna stood on the ridge that night, drinking a glass of wine. There was a rustling in the foliage nearby. For an instant, Laura's face became apparent among the trees.

Anna began slowly walking in the direction of the sound, surveying the sights around her.

Suddenly, a woman with blonde hair and brown eyes appeared in a robe and hood. Then more members of the Compendium appeared one after the other. Jason, Darren, Cindy, Alex, Bobby, Roy, the Cherokee girl, and all of the new and old members of the compendium walked silently through the woods in the direction of Jarret and Laura.

In her mind, Anna could hear Laura speaking, words perhaps intended to offer some manner of comfort.

Why does death never lie about?
Is it not listless on occasion,
disenchanted with its work,
disillusioned with the society of the departed?
Its stride is insidious constancy.
So many pass in this unchanging action,
yet the journey is always made alone.
Would not the blow be softened,
if we sat in a darkened cinema,
comfortable side by side in our chairs,

watched the screen fade to black,
and awakened to the second feature together?

Will's poetry, short stories, and guest blog articles have appeared in Half Tones to Jubilee, Riverwind, REAL: The Journal of Liberal Arts, Limestone, Cyclamens and Swords Magazine, Scrittura Magazine, California Quarterly, Off the Coast, On the Veranda, Orange Coast Review, Salmon Creek Journal, Ripples in Space, The Dead Mule School of Southern Literature, Theme Park Magazine, Submittable's Guest Blog, and the Institute of Internal Communication's Guest Blog.

Several of his feature screenplays have been under option to L.A. based production companies. Some of his short scripts have been produced, in addition to a pitch pilot for his reality series concept Haunted U.S.A. He wrote and co-directed a murder-mystery short film called The Victim that won the award for Best Professional Narrative Short Film at the UNA George Lindsey Film Festival. His scripts have also been successful in numerous screenplay competitions, including two recent Honorable Mention wins at the long running Screenplay Festival script competition and a Bronze Award at the L.A. Sci-Fi and Horror Festival.